ROUHR

CONQUERED WORLD: BOOK SIX

ELIN WYN

CLOCK
WALK
PUBLISHING

ROUHR

The first thing that hit me in the morning was a fresh stack of datapads.

I suspected that those who delivered reports strategically picked times they knew I wouldn't be in.

Perhaps I'd bring a cot into my office and sleep there from now on. It would save me the time of walking back and forth to my cabin and force the shy datapad deliverers to face me.

I shook the thought away and picked up the first datapad in the new stack. No surprise, it was from Thribb, as was the one underneath it. A quick glance told me they contained much of the same information as the one he'd dropped off in the late hours of last night.

I valued Thribb's council, as well as the information

he brought to my attention, but this was becoming excessive.

Time for something else.

The next contained a report from one of the evening guards who witnessed a small skirmish between two of the human refugees.

One stole the blanket of another, despite the fact she already had one of her own. An argument ensued, but the guard dispersed it, and the blanket was returned to its rightful owner.

That was something I'd noticed about humans. In times of crisis, they either banded together in a terrific show of support or turned on each other completely.

I was glad that the majority of the humans I'd met fell into the former category rather than the latter, though naturally there were a few exceptions.

As the unofficial leader of the refugees, I was sure Vidia Birch received a copy of this. She'd held a position of power in one of the first towns attacked by the Xathi, and the humans respected her.

Early on, we agreed that she'd handle the majority of the disciplinary actions in regard to the humans. It took a significant weight off my shoulders. It was only for serious offenses that I became involved, as it had been with Ren, the human Xathi informant.

I picked up the next in the stack.

Skrell.

Urai surveillance had shown that the Xathi mother ship was undergoing repairs. The damage that had been inflicted on it from its crash landing on the planet, as well as the battle that we had waged when killing the sub-queen, was in the process of being repaired.

Based on satellite photos, Fen and her team calculated that the Xathi ship would be spaceworthy in ten days.

When that happened, the slight advantage we had at this point over the Xathi would vanish.

The next report from the human doctor, Evie Parr, was far more hopeful. She was working on developing a cure to reverse the effects of hybridism.

The Xathi had infected the minds of a shockingly high number of humans, more than we'd ever seen before. The more control the Xathi held of the infected, the more Xathi-like they became.

Up until recently, we'd believed this was an irreversible condition.

Evie had been working practically around the clock since I'd sent her on a mission to the human city of Einhiv to study the condition.

The mission itself wasn't much of a success. Evie almost succumbed to hybridism in the process, but managed to escape it.

But not long ago, Evie had found a selection of naturally occurring chemicals in the brain that, when combined with certain chemical agents, affected the spread of hybridism. The datapad she left for me didn't contain news of a major breakthrough, as I'd hoped, just the details of a few small steps in the right direction.

I tried to keep my hopes realistic.

The Urai lab was more advanced than ours on the *Vengeance*, but even its resources were limited. I hoped Evie could find what she needed to solve this puzzle.

And now, there was no more avoiding it.

Time for Thribb.

Head Engineer Thribb was tasked with keeping me abreast of the *Aurora's* repair progress.

At present, the top priority was repairing the significant damage done to the *Aurora's* hull. It was almost completely split open on one side when the ship crash landed on the planet's surface after falling through a rift in space, a rift my men, and myself by extension, were responsible for creating.

Fen had also provided me with updates about the quickly improving structural integrity of the ship. Progress had nearly tripled since an ancient space-travel device known as the Gateway was found and recovered by a small team of humans, my men, and a Urai scientist.

The Gateway was able to stabilize the rift, and the Urai were able to funnel more power to the *Aurora*.

Now, the whole of the Urai's advanced technology was available to be used for repairs.

Thribb, however, had an ever-increasing list of other concerns, which he vocalized often. While he was pleased with the *Aurora's* progress, he now spent an inordinate amount of time calculating what would be required to make the ship efficient and safe for long-term space travel.

He, and a number of others, desired to leave the planet as soon as possible.

I understood their reasoning for that. According to his reports, available resources onboard were stretched thin between the humans and the crew. If we took on any more refugees, there would be even less to go around.

Still, there were camps of humans fleeing from the Xathi. Thribb knew I had every intention of opening up the *Aurora* to them if we found them, or if they found us.

Which brought up another of Thribb's many concerns: weight. When, or if, the *Aurora* was ready to fly again, the less weight she carried, the easier her journey would be.

Once, he had been bold enough to suggest that we dismiss any human that wasn't working toward the *Aurora's* repairs, but he received an instant reprimand from me.

The humans on this ship would be allowed to stay on this ship if they so chose, regardless of whether or not the *Aurora* ever flew again, regardless of their 'usefulness' to the mission.

And none of this addressed my growing concern: it didn't matter how many times I explained to Thribb that we didn't know if the *Aurora* would ever be fit for space travel again, he had convinced himself that she would be.

Ordinarily, I wouldn't tolerate it, but it seemed to be the only thing keeping Thribb going. Hope was harmless enough, and I wouldn't take that away from him.

Eventually, if his hopes were fulfilled, I'd have to make the choice of leaving this planet or staying on to help the humans.

The numbers all indicated that leaving was the most logical thing to do, but if it came down to it, could I bring myself to abandon the humans to the Xathi?

"General." A soldier appeared in the doorway to my office, a tinge of worry in his voice despite the ramrod posture.

"Is something the matter?" I set the datapad down.

"Xathi are approaching the *Aurora* from the south, sir."

"How many?"

"Less than ten, but they have a mass of hybrids with them. I couldn't get a clear count."

"Is the barrier holding?" Thus far, the sonic barrier surrounding the *Aurora* had yet to be extensively tested.

Recently perfected and tested in a few small-scale skirmishes with the Xathi and hybrids, the barrier projected the same frequency as our neurogrenades, only it was much stronger.

With the help of the Urai, we were able to perfect the technology that ensured a barrier of safety around the *Aurora*. The grenades were strong enough to disrupt a Xathi individual's connection to the hive-mind and the queen, causing some to roam aimlessly, others to spasm and collapse.

This was a variation of the barrier the *Aurora* had once used in space. Now it was a combination of the technology the *Vengeance* crew had devised, that the humans had added their expertise to, and the Urai had provided the missing link for—a true model of interspecies coordination and cooperation.

It had the ability to give us yet another advantage in our conflict with the Xathi.

In its first real test, I was curious to see how the barrier held up.

"Last I saw, the Xathi were still examining the barrier from a distance. It's possible they can sense the barrier," he reported.

"Mobilize ground teams A and C in front of where the Xathi were gathering." I ran over the rest of my schedule mentally.

Skrell it.

"I'll join you shortly."

The soldier nodded and walked away briskly.

In one of my larger desk drawers, I kept a blaster and a tactical vest. I tugged the vest on and strapped the blaster to my hip. If necessary, I could borrow a more powerful weapon from the one of the ground teams.

I hurried outside, expecting to be rushing into a firefight, but when I arrived, very little was happening.

"Report." I nodded to the leader of ground team A. He was a Valorni, as were the majority of the soldiers that made up the ground teams. Their superior strength made them ideal for hand-to-hand combat.

The leader pointed out that the Xathi were as close as they could get to the widest part of the tear in the hull.

"Only a few hybrids have attempted to cross the barrier, General. But none have been successful. It's killed some, but that doesn't appear to deter the others. The Xathi won't get close to it. I think they know what it will do to them."

"Odd. If they know they can't get through, then why bother?"

"Who can say?" the soldier shrugged.

"Perhaps it's about the Gateway," I mused. "Enough hybrids saw Daxion and Amira with it, the queen must be able to assume it's here. That might make a renewed attack worth the resources to her."

"Makes sense to me." He resumed his tense watch, waiting for a break in the pattern.

Another hybrid approached the barrier, this one so overgrown with crystals that it was hard to tell it was once human. My mind wandered to Evie and her cure.

Seeing that wretched creature before me diminished my hope that anything could be done for it.

Though the barrier itself was all but invisible, aside from the tall metal spikes that transmitted the sonic frequency, I could tell exactly when the hybrid came into contact with it. Its body went rigid, and it looked like it was trying to remove its head from its body. Eventually, it skittered backward, much to the displeasure of the observing Xathi.

"What should we do, General?"

After what I'd seen, I wasn't concerned about the Xathi getting through the sonic barrier, but they would make trouble when we eventually needed to go beyond the safety of the *Aurora*.

If a small team needed to deploy on a scouting mission, the Xathi would know exactly how many were in the team and where they were going.

If more joined the mob that had already gathered around the *Aurora*, we risked becoming trapped.

"Mobilize the strike teams. Tell them to load minimal ammo and see if they can clear this mess away." I gestured to the small mob of hybrids and Xathi. "Ground team A can return to their usual duties." The soldier nodded once and departed.

Thribb had been particularly up in arms about ammo conservation. I agreed that we did need to use it sparingly until we could craft suitable replacements, but driving off a mob certainly qualified as a just reason.

A figure appeared in the corner of my eye. I tried not to wince as he approached.

"General, a word?" Thribb appeared at my side.

I forced a smile and nodded for him to speak.

"I've been running calculations—"

"As always." Thribb laughed uncomfortably as I cut in.

"Yes, General. As always. I'm sure you know what I'm going to say."

"That it's imperative we vacate the planet as soon as possible?"

"Exactly." Thribb nodded. "The thing is, General, I don't believe you understand how dire our situation is becoming. I mean no disrespect."

"Yet, you've managed it." I tried to keep my

irritability in check. Thribb's people weren't big on social nuances. But this obsession of his was getting out of hand.

"Apologies. I've been allowed access to the Urai's interstellar maps. They're remarkably extensive. This is the first time I've gotten a clear picture of exactly where we are in the known universe. We are impossibly far from our home galaxy. The nearest planet suitable for landing will take a considerable amount of time for us to reach. We must start soon."

"How are you planning for us to make it home?" There was something terribly wrong with his reasoning, but he couldn't see it. "Or are you planning to use the Gateway?"

"We must leave immediately if we are to have any hope at all," he insisted. "The Gateway is still untested." He scowled. "Even if it does work, it only eliminates the concern for traveling distances. The Gateway cannot generate food, assist in emergency repairs, or maintain suitable oxygen levels and cabin pressure. We have what we need to maintain those things now, but the longer we linger on this planet, the less we will have when it comes time to leave."

"Yes, I believe you've told me that before." I tried not to grit my teeth.

"Then why haven't you—"

"Then why haven't I what? Abandoned the planet?

Abandoned a civilian population to whom we've brought a war? You insist that I don't understand, but I suspect it is you, Thribb, who doesn't understand. I know little of your people, but I cannot imagine them all to be as unfeeling as you have shown me you can be."

"It's my job to assure that our vessel, whichever vessel that may be, is fit for space travel and assure the safety of those on board. Your unwillingness to face reality," he waved his datapad which contained his multitude of calculations, "has made my job very difficult as of late."

"You're out of line." I never raised my voice when I was angry, but Thribb knew my temper was reaching its snapping point.

At least he had the decency to step back, even if he kept chattering. "It would go against my conscience to stay silent when you are putting the crew at serious risk. I believe you've become too emotionally invested, and that has marred your ability to make rational decisions, despite the overwhelming evidence that immediate evacuation is the only choice."

"You're dismissed, Thribb. Don't come to me again unless you've obtained new information."

"But, General—"

"Dismissed!"

Thribb left without another word.

I stood behind my men and watched the hybrids continuously try to move through the sonic barrier.

As much as I tried to put it out of my mind for the time being, there was something Thribb had said that stuck with me.

Many that I'd served under in the past preferred to leave their emotions out of the equation.

They claimed it made making difficult choices much easier.

Up until now, I'd strongly disagreed.

I believed becoming emotionally invested allowed the right decision to shine through more clearly.

However, this wasn't just a difficult decision—this was an impossible decision. I had to consider the fact that Thribb might have a point.

Perhaps this was a decision that needed to be made only with logic.

VIDIA

Between wrangling minor disputes between refugees, assigning quarters, and attempting to help locate missing family members from the Xathi attacks, lately I'd spent every moment of any spare time in the labs with Evie.

General Rouhr had said he'd give us as much time as possible to find a cure for the hybrids, but we all knew the clock was ticking.

Medical science and chemistry weren't my strong suits, so I'd enlisted Leena to assist Evie. With both of their capable hands, it was easier to run tests and analyze data, and I could wash bottles, carry, and fetch.

Anything to help.

Already, Leena had a few ideas. I didn't understand much of the technical talk, but essentially, Leena had a list of adjustments she could make to the synthetic chemicals she'd created to make them more efficient and effective than the naturally occurring brain chemicals Evie was experimenting with.

Evie and Leena made a fantastic team. They'd shared a lab on the *Vengeance* and were already accustomed to working with each other.

On Fen's recommendation, I'd brought in a Urai scientist named Glint, who had conducted several in-depth studies on the Xathi before landing on our planet.

Glint wasn't one for conversation, but from the excited chatter of Evie and Leena, she knew what she was doing and had filled in a missing piece of the puzzle.

At the moment, she was creating simulations on what a hybrid's brain chemistry looked like in various stages of infection. Once those simulations were complete, Leena and Evie could test their work.

The trio worked in harmony while I sat off to the side fidgeting, wishing there was more I could do.

"So, how long until we have a cure?" It'd been hours, at least, since I'd asked.

Evie sighed heavily and glared at me.

"If you ask me that one more time, I'm banning you from the lab. You know full well that this sort of thing doesn't run on a schedule. I could have a breakthrough in five minutes or five months."

I understood her testiness. There was a lot resting on her shoulders now.

"I know, I know." I put my hands up in surrender.

"It's actually not a bad thing that the hybrids keep flinging themselves at the sonic barrier, you know," Leena commented mildly. "Certainly, doesn't hurt that we have a steady supply of samples for testing."

"Leena," Evie gasped.

The chemist just shrugged. "You know I'm right. We can't work blind, and being soft-hearted isn't going to solve anything."

I could see that Evie didn't like it, but we all knew the truth. We needed every advantage we could possibly get, even if it was a tad... grisly.

"I don't understand why they're doing it, though," Leena added. "You'd think after they saw one die, they'd stop."

"I don't think they can control it." Evie would know better than any of us. Not long ago, she'd nearly lost her mind to the Xathi queen.

It still boggled my mind. "Then why would the Xathi queen force them into a barrier that would kill them? She must have realized she can't get to us."

"Maybe they're a distraction? She could be planning something bigger."

I agreed. "Still doesn't seem very logical."

"They're giant crystal bugs hell-bent on wiping out our population. Why are you looking for logic?" Leena gave a dry laugh.

"Because they're supposed to be military geniuses, too," I replied.

Evie amended that it could be a psychological thing. "She tried to manipulate me when she was in my head. She knows we know that the hybrids were once humans. Maybe she's just being spiteful by forcing so many to die in front of us."

"That's horrible." I shuddered.

"Hey, Leena! Come look at this." Evie was peering through a microscope.

Despite the topic of conversation, a smile bloomed over her features.

I took that as a good sign. Leena abandoned her work and peered through the microscope, too.

"That's great!" A smile appeared on her face, as well.

"What's great?" I didn't want to look through the microscope. I wouldn't understand what I was seeing.

"Hold on." Evie's excitement was growing by the second.

She gestured to Glint, who wasn't fond of using the speech-pad to talk, and asked her to look into the microscope, too. Glint silently analyzed whatever she was seeing. When she pulled away after a few minutes, she nodded at Leena and Evie with approval.

If she had a mouth, I guessed she'd be smiling.

"What is it?" I couldn't contain my curiosity. "Did you find a cure?"

"Not yet," Evie cautioned me. "But we're finally seeing the reaction we've been looking for. I think we've found the right combination of chemicals."

"So, what does that mean?" I asked.

Leena chimed in to explain that we needed to find the correct proportions. "We believe the Xathi queen alters the brain chemistry of a subject until it's shifted to a state that's compatible with hers. Once it's compatible, somehow she's able to take control, not only mentally, but by changing the body's physiology." She drummed her fingers on the workbench. "I'm not sure if we'll ever know exactly how she does that. But now, we have the correct mixture of natural and synthetic chemicals, so it could be possible for us to reverse the queen's damage."

"And that all means…" I prompted.

"We can potentially kick the Xathi queen out of someone's brain," Evie clarified.

"Incredible!" I clapped my hands together. "And you're sure?"

Leena opened her mouth, no doubt to launch into

another lengthy and technical explanation, but Evie cut in.

"Yes, we're sure." she grinned.

I couldn't wait to inform General Rouhr. I so hoped he'd be pleased. Like everyone else, I heard the swirl of rumor and worry that floated through the ship. I knew that soon he'd have to make some decisions. Hard ones.

Hopefully, this bit of good news would be enough to buy us more time, maybe give him some leverage. "Excellent work, ladies. I'll check in later."

I rushed out of the lab, excitement bubbling under my skin. Evie was so close. A cure could be days, maybe even hours, away.

Rouhr's office was empty when I checked for him, so I asked one of the guards stationed nearby. He wasn't on the *Aurora* at all, but on the ground outside. I thought that was strange, but I needed to speak with him immediately.

I took the elevator down to what we'd all started calling the ground floor. It wasn't the main hub of the *Aurora*, but it was where the tear in the hull lead right out to the ground.

I stepped back in surprise when I stepped out of the elevator. More than half of the rip in the hull was sealed up and in its final stages of repair.

At this rate, we'd need a new name for the level. I figured it wouldn't be long until the hull was completely finished and they could move on to repairing the engines and thrusters.

"General?" There were several soldiers stationed in front of the tear in the hull. They'd brought out storage crates to use as barricades, though they weren't taking any fire. Their guns and blasters, on the other hand, were aimed at the invisible wall that was the sonic barrier.

On the other side, I could see a large gathering of Xathi and hybrids. The Xathi still held back, while the hybrids charged right into the barrier. The frequency of the sonic barrier was calibrated to deter full Xathi.

I could only imagine what it was doing to the weaker hybrids, day after day. The sonic barrier didn't kill them right away, but that didn't stop the hybrids from running into it over and over.

Occasionally, one was strong enough to fight through the disruptive wavelengths. The soldiers immediately shot it down.

General Rouhr stood behind his men, surveying the damage.

"Wouldn't it be kinder to shoot them before they encounter the sonic barrier?" I couldn't help but ask.

"Kinder, perhaps," he nodded, eyes still fixed on the attackers. "But I'd rather watch and see if they learn to stop trying. Besides," his lips twisted into a half-smile, "we need to conserve ammo."

My shoulders slumped. "Evie thinks they don't have any control over their bodies."

"I'm inclined to agree with her. When they're exposed to those sonic wavelengths, they're essentially rattling their own brains."

I could've been mistaken, but I thought I detected pity in his voice.

"I've got some news that might cheer you up." I smiled. "Evie, Leena, and Glint have made an astounding breakthrough. A cure isn't far off."

"That's terrific." Rouhr's dark eyes glinted. "How long?"

"Evie almost threw me out for asking that question," I playfully warned Rouhr. "She can't give a timeline. It doesn't work that way. But it's only a matter of time."

The warmth drained from Rouhr's eyes. "Everything is a matter of time." There was a barrage of blaster fire as another hybrid managed to get past the barrier, though it was already falling before the first blast struck it. "I've made a decision."

"What's that?" Dread pooled in my stomach.

"As soon as the *Aurora* is flight-ready, my men and I are leaving." At least Rouhr had the courage to look me in the eyes when he told me. I'd give him that, but that's all I was going to give him.

"You can't be serious." I laughed, though nothing was funny. "I've just told you how close we are to

finding a cure, and you tell me you're abandoning us?"
Rage shot through my veins, white-hot and searing.

"I have to start thinking realistically." Rouhr's voice sounded infuriatingly calm and even. "I want to give you as much time as I can. But you said so yourself, Evie can't tell us when she'll have a cure. Thribb has told me when the *Aurora's* repairs will be complete, and I know how long we can sustain ourselves this way. We can't wait indefinitely for a cure that might not come in time."

"I'm not asking for you to wait indefinitely." My voice was rising. "I'm asking you to think about what your decision means for us."

"Night after night, it's kept me awake."

"Poor thing, I've been awake night after night, too, because the fate of my race was in the hands of someone else."

Rouhr opened his mouth to speak, but I cut in anyway, too angry to care about interrupting a general. An alien. Whatever.

"Do you realize what happens when you leave? Evie loses her lab. She loses every chance of finding a cure. Hundreds of people lose their food, shelter, and protection."

"I've offered the shelter of the *Aurora* indefinitely. That includes when we leave this planet."

"So that's the only choice we get? Abandon our

home or die? And what of the thousands that aren't on the *Aurora*? Don't they matter?"

"I have to think about my men." Rouhr's calm tone was cracking. "My men are trapped here while the Xathi are ravaging their homeworlds, too. Don't you think they deserve a say in where they go?"

That did it. I snapped.

"You're paying for your worlds with mine. There's a chance to save thousands and thousands of lives, and you're choosing not to take it. Justify it however you want, but that's the truth of the matter. Now, please excuse me."

I stormed away, leaving Rouhr standing among his soldiers with a scowl on his face and sadness in his eyes.

ROUHR

I hadn't slept in two days. Vidia's words echoed in my mind every moment of every day since we'd last spoken.

She was right.

I had allowed myself to mistake the logical decision for the right decision when I knew that, oftentimes, it was never that simple.

Vidia hadn't spoken more than a few sentences to me since I informed her of my decision, which wasn't surprising. We still had to interact often, since our jobs overlapped so much, but she avoided me as much as possible.

I knew how much she believed I'd do the right thing.

She'd put her faith in me, and I let her down.

I couldn't pin down why the thought bothered me so much, besides the obvious reason. It wasn't just that I'd be letting the humans down—it was that I'd be letting her down.

This was a war. War required sacrifices and difficult choices. I'd made a wrong choice, and if I could find a way to amend it, I would.

Vidia said there was always something to be done. I just needed to find something more substantial than a cure that might never come.

"General!"

I turned my head sharply toward the soldier who had called my attention. I could tell by his tone that it wasn't the first time he'd called me.

"Speak." I nodded.

"More Xathi and hybrids are arriving at the barriers. The strike teams have docked to restock their ammo."

"They're in the docking bay now?" The soldier nodded. "Tell them to come to the main conference room immediately, but only if you think the ground soldiers can handle the Xathi."

He confirmed that they could. "Hardly any actually make it through the sonic barrier. The Xathi don't even try. It's just the hybrids."

I paused, processing his statement. It suddenly made sense.

"Call out the snipers to join the ground crew, except

for Tu'ver. But I'll send him out after the strike team meeting. Replace the entire ground team with snipers if you can."

"Sir?" the soldier confirmed.

"The Xathi aren't trying to attack. They're just trying to get us to waste our ammo. Snipers will take out the hybrids in one shot. Make sure they know to conserve as much as possible." The soldier nodded his head once and walked away.

I made my way to the larger conference room one deck up. It didn't take long for my crew to arrive.

They looked confused. I'm sure they were wondering why I'd pulled them from combat. It was strange to think that the Xathi were so close to us, but couldn't reach us.

Once everyone I'd asked for was present, I spoke.

"I formed your strike teams long ago as a way to reward the best and brightest of my soldiers and to make sure superior forces could be sent where they were needed most. Today, I've called you in for a different and somewhat unusual reason."

"Is this about the *Aurora* repairs?" Vrehx asked.

"It is." I nodded. "Thribb and I have been meeting regularly for some time now, as I'm sure you all know."

"We know Thribb wants to leave," Sakev scoffed. "Can't think about anything else."

"And you don't?" Karzin shot back.

Sakev was going to say something back, but I cleared my throat. All attention was drawn back to me.

I ran my ship differently than most other generals. My crew didn't need permission to speak. They were free to voice their thoughts.

I believed that, because of that, the respect my crew had for me was genuine. I didn't demand respect, then punish them when it was withheld. I sought to earn it. I believed it made all the difference.

But this was still my meeting, and it would run to my time.

"Thribb continuously runs calculations, measuring everything from ammunition to refugee resources. Finding the Urai and saving the *Aurora* was a stroke of luck. It's much better equipped to house refugees than the *Vengeance* was. What it lacks in defense weaponry, it makes up for in its technology, like the sonic barriers."

"General, you're not saying you prefer this luxury cruise liner to the *Vengeance*, are you?" Sk'lar lifted a brow.

I gave a short chuckle.

"I wouldn't go that far," I replied. "The *Vengeance* was designed to fight the Xathi. That's what we need. However, I think we all know the *Vengeance* isn't likely to fly again. The *Aurora*, on the other hand, has a much better chance."

"The hull is nearly repaired," Axtin interjected. He'd

been one of the first to see the *Aurora* when she crash-landed. "But do you think she'll fly again? That's two entirely different things."

"From the reports, I have high hopes," I answered honestly. The repairs were going more smoothly than I would've guessed.

"So, is that it, then?" Rokul spoke up. "The *Aurora* will likely fly again, and when she does, we can finally pack up and get back to the real fight."

"This *is* a real fight," Tu'ver said through gritted teeth.

"This is one Xathi ship targeting a small civilian population. Back in our galaxy, there are hundreds of ships ravaging our worlds as we speak—our homes, remember? I'd consider that a higher priority," Rokul shot back.

At this point, I took a step back and listened. This was the sort of open discussion I'd been hoping to elicit. This was when I learned the most about the crew.

If things got out of hand, I'd step in. But these unfiltered discussions were more informative than anything else.

"It's our fault the Xathi are here. It's our responsibility to deal with them," Vrehx remarked.

"It's *your* fault," Karzin emphasized. "It was on your order that an experimental weapon was fired, tore a hole in the universe, and brought us here, away from the real war."

Vrehx's eyes were murderous, but he knew better than to resort to violence.

"It doesn't matter whose fault it is," Sk'lar argued. "We're not going to abandon a civilian population to the Xathi. It's against everything we stand for."

"I joined up to protect *my* people on *my* world," Rokul interjected. "I have sisters and a mother that need my protection, and I'm no good to them if I'm stuck here." His brother, Takar, echoed his sentiments.

Axtin rolled his eyes upon hearing this. "We all have families to worry about."

"Not all of us," Sakev muttered.

But Karzin wasn't one who would easily back down. "Just because some of you don't have anything to go back to, it doesn't mean I want to trade the lives of my family for the lives of these humans, galaxies away from home."

"Enough." I raised one hand. The crew went silent, though I could still feel their anger radiating off them. "It would seem that you have some mixed feelings on the subject of leaving. Not a surprise. Let's turn the discussion to solving a problem, rather than arguing about it."

"What's there to solve? This isn't our planet. This isn't our problem," Karzin stubbornly insisted.

Whether or not I agreed, I did understand his frustration.

Some of the crew knew for a fact that their loved ones had been killed in the initial Xathi attacks on our respective worlds.

Karzin was one of many who didn't know if his family was alive or not, which was arguably worse.

I hadn't been able to receive any reports from other units concerning the state of our home planets before we fell through the rip, but I remember when the Xathi first appeared.

They were quick to kill and destroy.

On my planet, they knew exactly where to strike to hurt us the most. I'm sure it was the same for the other planets.

I wouldn't dare say this out loud. I hated to even think it.

But if we did return to our homeworlds, I doubted there would be much left to return *to*.

"Even if the *Aurora* is ever declared fit for space travel," Tu'ver spoke over Karzin, "I can tell you now, I won't be on it. I'll be staying here. I'll fight for the humans, regardless."

"As will I," Vrehx seconded.

Nearly half of the strike teams declared they would willingly stay behind even if the *Aurora* was cleared for space travel. There was a clear trend. All who agreed to stay had grown close to the humans while they were here, joined by many of those who knew they had no family back home to defend.

It was no secret that some of my crew had found love in the arms of human women. Many had also built strong friendships.

Those who were adamant about leaving hadn't socialized much with the humans. They'd likely avoided contact on purpose, knowing we'd have to leave at some point.

This divide presented a whole new slew of problems. If the *Aurora* left Ankau, it would be leaving without many vital crewmembers.

I'd need Thribb to factor that into his unending calculations. He'd probably be thrilled at the challenge.

"What of the cure for hybridism?" Daxion spoke up. "How does that change things?"

"It's progressing," I replied. "Not as quickly as I'd like, but there's nothing to be done about that."

"Evie's working night and day to make it happen," Sakev growled. "She doesn't rest, even when I tell her to."

"I know she is," I agreed. "It's simply a matter of time. A cure needs to be produced before we leave on the *Aurora*."

"So, the *Aurora* will leave, if she's able?" Karzin insisted.

"As of this moment, that's in our best interest," I announced. "However, the development of a cure could change or forestall that."

"That'd be even more of a reason to leave," Rokul said. "If they can cure the hybridism, the humans will have more people available to fight against the Xathi. They won't need us."

"That's not for you to decide," I corrected. "I've given you all of the information I have at present. You're all dismissed, but let me warn you now," I added before they could slip off, "should I hear of any arguing or similar conduct over today's discussion outside of this room, there will be consequences." I didn't lift my gaze until I received a nod of understanding from everyone.

When they'd all gone, I lowered myself into the closest seat.

I enjoyed meeting regularly with the crew. These meetings usually provided a sense of clarity.

But now I had just confirmed that the crew was as torn about this as I was.

A headache pulsed at my temple.

Of all things, I was craving the humans' coffee.

And maybe a sympathetic ear to share it with. But Vidia still wasn't talking to me, so coffee alone it would be.

VIDIA

I was in the lab again, for once not badgering Evie and Leena with questions about the cure every five minutes. They enjoyed the silence at first, but after a few hours of it, they realized something wasn't right.

During the day, I usually sat at my desk in the refugee wing so I could talk to people if they needed something.

However, for the past three days, I'd been hiding out in the lab. I didn't know how I could face everyone, knowing that Rouhr was planning on leaving Ankau.

I'd have to tell everyone sooner or later.

The news would have to come from me.

If it came from Rouhr or any of the alien crew members, there'd be a riot.

I just needed a little bit more time to work up my nerve.

How could I look into a sea of trusting faces and tell them their choice was either to abandon their home or to stay on a planet swarming with Xathi?

I was still furious with Rouhr.

Mostly.

Entirely.

But yet...the small part of me that wasn't angry with him understood his point of view, but I could never support his decision.

"Your silence is creeping me out." Evie peered up at me from her lab table.

"I've got a lot to think about."

I had to keep reminding myself that nothing was final yet. There was still time for Evie, Leena, and Glint to find a cure. If they did, Rouhr would have to change his mind about leaving right away.

Then again, there was always the chance that he wouldn't.

I was so engrossed in thought that I didn't hear the shouting at first.

"Vidia!" Evie shouted my name, bringing me back to the here and now. I snapped to attention.

"What is it? What's the matter?" I scrambled to my feet. I looked at Evie. There were tears in her eyes.

"We did it!"

It was then that I saw a huge smile plastered on her face. "Did what?" I was still convinced something terrible had happened.

"The cure, Vidia!" Evie exclaimed. "We did it!"

Finally, the pieces clicked together in my head. Happy tears. Evie was crying happy tears. The shouts were shouts of joy, not yet another imminent disaster.

Still, it was hard to hope. "Are you sure?"

"Come see for yourself!" Evie gestured to her microscope.

"Will what I see make a bit of sense to anyone without medical training?"

"Not in the slightest." Evie laughed.

Slowly, bit by bit, a tremendous weight began to lift from my chest and shoulders. I took what felt like my first full breath in days.

We had a cure for hybridism. It was finally sinking in.

"How does it work?" I inquired.

"It can easily be made into an airborne...purifier." Evie searched for the right word. "However, it wouldn't be hard to condense it into pill form for people to take orally."

"Incredible." I clasped my hands together in front of my chest. "We've got to bring this to Rouhr immediately."

I waited for Leena, Evie, and Glint to gather the notes and test results they wanted Rouhr to see.

"Do you want to do the talking, Evie?" I asked.

"No," Evie answered quickly, her eyes widening. "I always get so nervous talking to the general."

"Whatever for?" I held back a laugh.

"He's the only one on this ship scarier than Axtin or Leena," Evie murmured.

We both glanced at Leena.

"Axtin? Scary?" she snorted. "But you're right, the general is an intimidating figure."

Odd words, coming from Leena, who steadfastly refused to be afraid of anything or anyone.

Odd altogether, really. I'd never found Rouhr particularly intimidating. Up until recently, I'd held him in the highest regards, but I was never intimidated by him.

"I'll do the talking, then. I suppose." I didn't bother hiding my confusion.

"It makes sense, considering you're the human female version of him." Leena shrugged.

"I am?" This was news to me.

"How have you not noticed?" Evie laughed. "You two are practically the same person, only you have twice the energy."

"Do you think I'm intimidating?" I asked.

Evie and Leena both took a moment to consider,

while Glint listened in with what I could guess was an amused expression on her face.

"I respected you right away," Evie answered. "But I think you're less intimidating than Rouhr."

"He's a giant red alien covered in battle scars, after all," Leena added.

"He's only got the one scar," I corrected.

I don't know why it was so important for me to mention that. Rouhr probably did have scars in other places that I couldn't see.

Not that I thought about it often...or at all.

Really.

The one on his face wasn't that bad. Yes, it was noticeable, and it was clearly from a bad injury, but I thought it added even more ruggedness to him. He must have been one hell of a soldier before he moved into an office.

I forced myself to stop thinking about Rouhr and his life. I was still angry with him. Though, hopefully, once he found out we had a cure for the hybridism, I wouldn't have to be angry with him anymore.

When we left the lab, I was practically running. I reached Rouhr's office long before the others did. I peeked through the office window while I waited for them to catch up.

Rouhr sat at his desk, looking exhausted.

Too many nights I'd gone to bed late, and could see his lights still on.

I'd guess he still wasn't sleeping at night.

Thribb stood in front of the desk, gesturing broadly as he spoke.

I would've preferred to announce the cure to Rouhr when he was alone, but it wouldn't hurt for Thribb to know, either. There were options, ramifications, whether the single-minded engineer wanted to acknowledge them or not.

I waited for the others to catch up before I knocked.

To be honest, Rouhr looked relieved to have an excuse to interrupt Thribb. He spotted me through the window, and his expression shifted between surprise and concern.

"Vidia, is everything all right?" he asked when he opened the door.

"They found a cure," I announced.

A broad smile spread across Rouhr's face. It was a nice smile, a genuine smile.

It made him even more handsome.

"You're certain?" He looked from me to the others, then back at me.

"The simulations we ran produced incredible results," Evie piped up.

"Simulations?" Thribb turned to us. "You've only tested this *cure* via simulations?"

"It's not like we can bring a live hybrid on board for testing," Leena interjected. "These simulations are almost as good as the real thing. Glint is an expert, after all." Leena nodded to Glint, who nodded back.

"*Almost* is the difference between life and death, success and failure, with these sorts of things," Thribb argued. "What you really have is a mash-up concoction of who knows what with no real evidence that it works."

"Enough, Thribb," Rouhr warned.

I'd never spoken much to Thribb. We often attended the same meetings with Rouhr and others, but we'd never had reason to speak with each other. I was shocked by his immediate rejection of the cure.

"Apologies," Thribb muttered, but his callousness was the end of my patience.

"No." My temper snapped like the end of a bullwhip. "I want to know why you're objecting so strongly without even looking at the data Evie, Leena, and Glint have spent days gathering."

"The *Aurora* and her repairs must take first priority," he said smugly. "To utilize the cure would mean taking resources away from the repairs. I'm assuming you four weren't planning on marching through Xathi territory yourselves, handing it out like a treat, hmm?"

"You know that's not possible," I replied.

"Exactly. So, you'd need teams, transport units,

ammunition, and likely even more to spread this cure. Yet, this cure hasn't been tested. There's a chance—no doubt, you're going to tell me it's a small chance—that the cure will be useless, resulting in a waste of already limited resources." Thribb folded his spindly arms over his narrow torso.

"There's a chance of error in your calculations, though I'm sure you'll tell me it's a small one, yet you're parading those as infallible," I shot back.

"The programs and systems I use to make my calculations have the smallest error percentage in the known universe," he snapped.

"Do you use the Urai's tech for your work?" I asked.

"Of course," he scoffed. "Everything of mine was left back on the *Vengeance*."

"So, somehow the Urai tech you're using is superior to the tech that Glint, a Urai herself, was using to painstakingly construct a realistic simulation of how the cure would interact with the brain chemistry of a hybrid?" I challenged.

"My methods are tried and tested. Glint's simulations were created from scratch and yet to be tested until this day," Thribb argued.

"Just admit that you're a coward and you're trying to convince the general to run away!" I snapped.

"Vidia," Rouhr said gently. My focus was pulled from Thribb, and my anger was able to dissipate. Rouhr had one arm extended in my direction, his hand open and hovering a few inches over my forearm.

"I'm sorry," I sighed. "Your engineer hasn't heard of empathy."

"The facts force me to look beyond empathy," Thribb replied.

Rouhr shot him a warning look.

I didn't want to say anything at that moment, especially since I'd never seen the calculations Thribb often cited, but I had a difficult time believing the situation was as dire as Thribb insisted it was.

Down in the refugee wing, it was common courtesy not to take more than what was needed. But even then, there was always more than enough to go around. If the *Aurora* was under that much strain, I felt like we would feel it more in the refugee wing.

But, again, I'd never seen Thribb's calculations, so I stayed quiet.

For now.

Rouhr read over Evie and Glint's notes. It didn't take him long to skim through the most vital bits of information.

"Since it's my decision," Rouhr began, looking at Thribb out of the corner of his eye, "curing the affected humans is now the top priority."

I expected Thribb to argue, but he stayed silent. Maybe he actually would care, after all.

But he wasn't my concern.

"Thank you." I placed my hand on Rouhr's shoulder, "You're doing the right thing."

Even through his jacket, the heat of his skin tingled through my fingers. I pulled away sharply, but not before our eyes met.

What on earth was that?

ROUHR

I called a meeting the following morning and watched the members of my strike teams file in.

Silent.

Tense.

My crew knew me well enough to know I only called multiple meetings in a week if something big was going to happen.

"I'm sure some of you have heard by now."

I glanced at Axtin and Sakev. I had a reasonable suspicion that Leena and Evie had revealed their breakthrough to their mates.

"A cure for hybridism has been developed. As I told you last time we met, this does affect our plans with the *Aurora*."

Several team members swore under their breath, apparently under the false impression that the dulling color of my scales also indicated my hearing was going.

I shot Rokul and Karzin warning looks, and they straightened sharply in their chairs.

Neither had been shy about voicing their opinions in the past, but this wasn't the time.

"I should hope that, as the best and brightest of my crew, you remember the oath you took," I continued, my mild tone offsetting the dead seriousness of my words. "When we last met, I heard your concerns and your respective opinions. However, now we have a chance to save a great many lives. If you still feel strongly against pouring our time and energy into attempting to reverse the hybridism, then, by all means, you may leave this room."

A small percentage of the strike teams began to shift in their seats.

"However," I added before anyone could move too much, "you will be breaking your oath and will be demoted."

Those who were considering leaving quickly stilled.

"Very good," I grinned.

That should take care of any insubordination. "Vidia, would you like to share your thoughts?"

She stepped forward, her calm bearing once again

impressing me. A few months ago, none of her people had ever had contact with another intelligent space-faring species.

Now she faced a room of alien warriors, not all of whom were thrilled to hear her news, as easily as she settled random disputes between the humans.

I forced my wandering attention back to her words, rather than her interestingly expressive face.

"At this moment, Dr. Parr and Dr. Dewitt have returned to the lab to perfect their innovation. Dr. Parr has informed me that the cure can be produced in two different forms. For the time being, I'd like to focus on the airborne form."

She rattled off the technical details. Obviously, she'd prepared thoroughly for the presentation; as usual, being her people's voice so that the scientists could get on with their work.

She must have crammed all night. I smothered a grin. I'd have had to do the same for something so far outside my regular scope.

"It will be easy for you to tell where the airborne variation has been released," she continued. "The gas has been colored bright pink, so that there's no wasted time wondering where the cure has been deployed."

"Excuse me, did you say pink?" Axtin interrupted. He sounded like he was trying not to laugh.

"I did," Vidia confirmed, "Why?"

"That was Leena's choice, wasn't it? She has a thing for pink," he replied.

Vidia cracked a smile. "You'll have to ask her." She refocused, concluding the presentation. "Due to the nature of the airborne cure, the scientific team agrees that a highly concentrated air strike would be the best course of action. Is this something that would be possible?" Vidia looked to me.

"Sounds entirely possible," I replied. "Strike team leaders, do you agree?" Vrehx, Sk'lar, and even Karzin nodded their agreement.

"Excellent." I clapped my hands together. "Last night, I took it upon myself to gather some information on the daily patterns of the hybrids. Fen and her surveillance equipment proved to be most helpful. It appears that the hybrids don't reside on the Xathi ship with the queen. Instead, they are kept in camps closely monitored by a handful of Xathi guards."

"You really don't sleep, do you?" Vidia looked at me with a mix of horror and admiration.

Despite her obvious preparations for the presentation, Vidia seemed more rested than she often did. Perhaps the good news had given her easier sleep.

Her dark hair looked shinier, and her uniquely hued eyes looked brighter. I'd never seen a human with eyes like hers before, halfway between blue and purple. The humans called the shade violet.

Unique. Fascinating.

"What's the purpose of these camps?" Tu'ver asked. I snapped my attention back where it belonged. The mission. The war. "Why would the Xathi bother keeping the hybrids separate?"

"I have some thoughts on that." I laced my fingers together, sweeping my gaze over the teams. Now that a decision had been made, a clear target presented, they were unified in their attitudes once again.

"The largest camps are placed near cities that still have a big enough population to infiltrate and turn into hybrids. One is near Glymna, the only major city that the Xathi haven't attacked head-on. That should be our first mark. As for why the Xathi are living separately from the hybrids," I shook my head. "It's my guess that the Xathi are using the hybrids as cannon fodder. Usually, Xathi can signal the others in the hive-mind and call in virtually unlimited reinforcements. That's not the case here. They're cut off from the rest of their armada. We've already speculated that their mental connection can't cross the rift. Even if there are other Xathi on their way, they won't be arriving any time soon."

"Could others come here?" Vidia's face was a shade

paler than it had been before. "Other Xathi could attack Ankau?"

I assured her that there were no signs of them on any of the Urai scanners. "Believe me, if there were more coming, we'd know."

She nodded, but I could still see some worry on her brow. I pulled out a palm-sized projector from my pocket and placed it on the table, so it could project a map of the hybrid camps on the wall.

"So, the camp near Glymna first." Vrehx stood up to examine the projection. "The camp near Duvest seems like a good next step. There's still a decent-sized civilian population there. The one near the *Vengeance* can be hit last. There shouldn't be too many people out there."

"Why would they be near the *Vengeance*?" Rokul asked.

"I bet they're waiting on us to come back," Dax replied.

Sour mutters rounded the room. None of us liked the idea of our ship, our home, being used to bait us.

"Hybrids routinely go on patrols," Sakev commented. "If we do this right, we can lure some of the patrols to the camps and lump them in with the others when we drop the cure."

"Does the cure have any effect on the Xathi themselves?" Sk'lar asked.

"As far as I understand, no," Vidia answered. "It works by altering brain chemistry, so the brain in question has to be a human one underneath the modifications that have been done by the queen."

"At what point do the hybrids' brains stop resembling a human's?" Tu'ver asked. "At what point is the cure not effective because the human has been too modified?"

"That's something we're going to find out for ourselves." Vidia bit her lip, knowing that the probable answer wasn't going to end well. "Evie doesn't have many brain scans of infected humans, especially ones that have been changed so far. She can only extrapolate."

"Once the cure is deployed into the hybrid population, what happens next?" Vrehx wondered.

"It won't take much airpower to deploy the cure, therefore the majority of you will be with ground units ready to deal with the Xathi guards," I explained. "The cure should start to work immediately, but if it doesn't, do your best not to harm any of the hybrids."

"What if the cure doesn't take hold right away or doesn't work at all?" Karzin said.

"Then I trust each of you to act with your best judgment," I replied. "But remember, this is officially considered a rescue mission, so only kill the hybrids if it's absolutely necessary. If the cure works as we hope it will, there will be a lot of confused and scared people. We will be using holo-disguises for these missions, so we don't cause further panic. I urge you to see things from their point of view and act accordingly. Understood?" There was a collective nod.

Despite their concerns, they were good men. They'd do the right thing.

"What happens after that?" Axtin leaned back in his chair, a distant look on his face.

"There will be a re-acclimatization process for those who were successfully rescued," I explained. "Though that won't be your responsibility. That will fall to Vidia and her people."

"No, I mean after that," Axtin corrected. "After we've completed the rescue mission and saved the humans?"

Not exactly a conversation I wanted to have right now, but I'd picked the best and brightest. Which meant there'd never be a shortage of questions, I supposed.

"There are more hybrids than there are Xathi," I began slowly. "With the hybrid population thinned and our fighting population bolstered, it's possible that we will be able to take the Xathi in battle."

"You want the rescued humans to fight the Xathi?" Vidia looked at me with alarm, though she tried to hide it.

"Only if they're willing and able," I clarified. "If you

had your mind taken away from you and managed to get it back, wouldn't you want to stop the one responsible for taking it in the first place?"

"I suppose I would," Vidia considered, her words hesitant as she considered it.

"Once the Xathi are defeated, will we be able to leave?" Karzin asked.

Of course he did.

"If this planet has been saved from the Xathi, and the if *Aurora* is deemed safe for long-term space travel, I see no reason why we couldn't return to our homeworlds," I answered.

Out of the corner of my eye, I thought I saw Vidia's small shoulder sag a little bit.

"Will we be ordered to return?" Vrehx asked.

"If you wish to resign from this crew to stay behind, I will not stop you," I responded.

Every strike team member looked more pleased than they had when they entered the room. There was a way forward, both for those who wished to remain, and those who wished to return home.

If everything worked according to plan.

And I'd seen too many battles to bet on that. However, it was the best I could offer them. The best I could offer any of us.

"If there are no further questions, you're dismissed.

I'll send an alert when it's time for the first strike to take place."

"Did that go well?" Vidia asked once only she and I remained in the room.

"You know it did." I gave her a wry smile. "It would appear that we're all on the same team once more."

"It would seem so." She smiled up at me for a moment before looking away. "I need to go check on Evie and Leena. They'll be pleased with the results of this meeting."

I wanted to say something more to her, but I didn't know what. I let her leave the conference room.

This had turned out better than I could've hoped for just a few days ago.

Once the planet was saved, my crew and I could go home, neat and tidy.

Everyone wins.

I wouldn't go as far as to say I'd grown fond of this planet. The people residing on it?

Yes, I'd grown fond of many of them.

The creatures that lived on this planet were a different story entirely. I enjoyed a good fight as much as the next Skotan, but it was quite another thing to need to bring a full arsenal for a walk amongst the trees.

I loved my home planet.

I missed the soaring peaks of the red mountains and the cities hidden under the planet's crust.

Yet somehow the idea of leaving this place and going home didn't bring a smile to my face.

And a certain violet gaze had nothing to do with that.

Of course not.

VIDIA

"Do you think there's such a thing as too much of this cure?" I wondered aloud.

Evie had given me a list of very specific, impossible-to-fuck-up instructions as to how to make the cure in its concentrated liquid form.

She was beside me doing the same, our mini assembly line working as quickly and carefully as possible to be ready for the first strike.

"It restores brain chemistry," Evie said. "I don't think it can make a brain too human."

"Superhuman!" Leena exclaimed from where she was adding a chemical compound that strengthened the effects of the base mixture Evie and I were making.

"What?" I laughed.

"You don't know what the Superhumans are?" Leena

gasped. She looked at Jeneva, who was flipping through her field guides, searching for any natural substances that could improve the cure.

"Don't look at me! I have no idea what you're talking about," she shrugged, and went back to her files.

"Are Mariella and I the only ones who had a proper childhood?" Leena exclaimed. She twisted around to speak to her sister, who sat with Amira on the other side of the lab. "Mariella, they don't know about the Superhumans."

Mariella looked up from the map projection she was studying. "You're not serious!" She looked at each of us, waiting to be let in on the joke.

"We're serious," Evie replied without looking up from her work.

"Are you going to tell us, or are you just going to keep gaping at us for not knowing?" I poured all of my concentration into releasing the exact right amount of one of the chemical components from the pipette in my hand.

"It was a TV series back on Earth," Mariella explained. "Our great-grandmother brought some of the videos here. We used to watch them over and over again when we were kids."

"It was about a group of seemingly regular people, but they all had these crazy powers," Leena added. "Like one of them was even stronger than Axtin and another one could turn invisible if she wanted to."

"My favorite Superhuman could stop time, but she would still be able to move," Mariella recalled. "She would freeze time if someone was about to fall or die and move them somewhere safe."

"I'd like that power," I remarked. "Imagine how much work I could get done." Evie chuckled beside me.

"Did they just walk around, randomly helping people?" Amira asked.

"They were part of a secret team," Mariella explained. "They worked together to stop evil Superhumans from taking over cities or destroying the planet."

"Now that sounds a little too familiar." Evie laughed. "Do you still have the videos? Maybe we could take notes."

"We kept them down in the basement of our old house," Leena recalled. "I bet they're still there."

"We'll have to go dig them out once we take care of the bug problem," I commented.

"Speaking of the bug problem," Amira interjected, "Vrehx suggested attacking the camp near Glymna first, right?"

"Yes," I confirmed. "Why?"

"First, I think we should use the Gateway for the strikes so none of the Xathi surrounding the *Aurora* can spot our direction in the air and warn the others. Second, if they'd come at the camp from the East, I doubt the Xathi guards would see it coming," she said. "They wouldn't be expecting anything to come at them from the direction of the city."

"That's a good idea, but look what I found." Mariella pushed a datapad in Amira's direction. "Hardly any of the crew knows how to take proper notes. It's infuriating."

Amira agreed. "I'm not even sure what they're talking about." She flipped the data-pad over as if she thought she was reading it upside down.

"They're patrol notes," Mariella explained. "Those messy scrawls are coordinates that, I think, correspond with where our patrols crossed the paths of hybrid patrols."

"Sakev had the idea of using the air units to lure any patrols closer to the camps so we won't have to hunt them down later," I added.

"It's a good idea," Mariella agreed. Evie seemed pleased. "Though we'd lose the element of surprise."

"I think dropping pressurized canisters of exploding pink mist after appearing through a rift is going to be surprising enough." Amira laughed, then straightened up, head tilted to the side. "I have to ask, why are we doing this? Shouldn't this sort of strategizing be left to the professionals?"

I realized the question was directed at me.

"Not all of the crew members were happy that the *Aurora's* departure is going to take the backseat to our rescue mission," I answered.

"You don't think anyone will give us any trouble, do you?" Jeneva asked.

Honestly, I didn't think so. "Rouhr gave them a good reason not to disobey his orders on this one."

"And we have a lot of muscle on our side," Leena added.

I noticed that talking about the *Aurora's* departure didn't bother the others the way it bothered me.

I assumed their mates already told them they weren't going to leave Ankau, leave them behind.

Even though I'd gotten what I wanted in the end, the idea of the *Aurora* departing after the Xathi were handled made me feel unhappy.

Rouhr had said time and time again that there was the possibility that the *Aurora* would never be able to travel through space again.

Secretly, I felt guilty for hoping that would be the case, especially when I didn't want to think too much about the reasons why.

So many of the crew missed their homeworlds. They wanted to return, to find their families, and to do what they could to win the war that would rage long after they left our world. I couldn't blame them for that.

It was selfish of me to want something like that for myself if it meant heartache for so many others.

"I expect Thribb will try to block our mission." I pulled myself away from my current train of thought.

"Really?" Mariella's brow furrowed.

Leena recalled how irritated Thribb had been when they told General Rouhr about the cure. "He didn't like that Vidia challenged the accuracy of his calculations."

"I didn't like that he challenged the accuracy of Glint's," I replied.

I looked over to Glint, who worked quietly in the back of the room. She was taking the final mixtures and putting them through a machine that converted the small amount of liquid and turned it into a medical vapor stored in a pressurized canister. She didn't have her speech pad, so she couldn't speak to us, but I was sure she was listening to every word.

"I'm sure he's under a lot of pressure," Mariella offered. She always tried to see the best in people.

Mariella was probably right. Probably.

"But I still want to have as many bases covered as possible, so no one has the option of poking holes in this mission. Between all of us, we know as much about the terrain, the Xathi, and the cure as anyone else on this ship. More."

A round of nods answered me.

"Besides, the more work we do now, the less Rouhr

will have to scramble to get everything together. He has enough on his plate as it is."

"That's sweet." Evie smiled.

"What's sweet?" I asked.

"You're concerned about the general," she replied.

"I'm not being sweet," I countered. "I'm being a decent human being. Anyone can see that he's overworking himself. I've never seen him out of his office for more than a few hours at a time. Do Skotans need less sleep than humans?"

"Sakev sleeps more than I do." Evie laughed.

"Vrehx is really, terrifyingly consistent with his sleep schedule," Jeneva added. "He prefers to go to bed and wake up at the exact same time every day, and he's grumpy as hell if he doesn't. He still needs at least six hours, though."

"Exactly," I said. "I don't think Rouhr gets anywhere near that much."

"Neither do you," Evie averred.

"Yeah, but I'm not a general," I replied.

"You care!" Evie teased. "Just admit it! There's nothing wrong with caring. It's what you're known for, anyway."

"Really? I thought I was known for never letting things be," I joked, an uncomfortable feeling spreading in my chest.

"Oh, you're known for that, too," Evie laughed.

"Speaking of not letting things be, there's one thing I can't work out," I added, ready for a new topic.

"What's that?"

"How many people are we going to have to shelter?" I inquired.

"I've been thinking about that, too." Evie nodded. "It's impossible for us to know exactly how many people were affected by the hybridism, and we have no way to know how many of the affected still have a somewhat-human brain."

"Wouldn't it be the ones who were infected first that have the least-human minds?" Mariella queried.

"That seems logical, doesn't it?" Evie replied. "But when I was studying the virus in Einhiv, I encountered strains that could take over a person in less than a day, as well as strains that were so slow-acting that the person infected had no idea they were a carrier."

"Do you think the Xathi queen has some sort of direct influence over how the hybridism spreads?" Amira speculated.

"It wouldn't surprise me," Evie shrugged. "Though if she could, that wouldn't explain why she didn't try her hardest to steal my mind."

"Maybe she tried her hardest, and you're just stronger than you think." I rubbed Evie's shoulder.

"Thanks, Mom," Evie stuck out her tongue.

"You're welcome," I teased. "Unfortunately, I still

don't have a clue as to how many more people we're going to get."

"If this cure works like I hope it will, it's going to be a lot," Evie said.

"I'm going to go talk to Rouhr," I remarked. "He can tell me how many more people we can take on. It'll be better than trying to ask Thribb." I pushed away from the lab table and slipped out of the white coat I'd borrowed from Evie.

"Don't forget to tell him how much you care," Evie teased.

"I'm not going to do that." I rolled my eyes.

"Aha! You admit it!" Leena exclaimed.

"I didn't admit anything." I busied myself putting away the lab coat, trying to ignore the heat rising in my cheeks.

"You admitted that there's something to admit!" Evie replied.

"No, I didn't. You just have an overactive imagination," I maintained. I walked over to where Amira and Mariella were sitting.

"Can I show Rouhr what you've come up with so far?" I asked.

"Sure." Mariella handed over the datapad she'd been working on. "Be sure to tell him to teach his crew how to take better field notes."

"I can do that." I laughed.

"You'll criticize him, but you won't tell him you're worried about his sleep schedule?" Evie lifted a brow. "You must be in love."

"That's the silliest thing I've heard all day." I shook my head. "It makes no sense. I'm not in love with anyone, for your information. I'm going to go be productive now."

I waggled my fingers at them as I left the lab.

In love.

Really.

ROUHR

Vidia always knocked four times in quick succession, lighter than anyone else in the crew. Other than Thribb, but he rarely knocked anymore. Vidia's interruption was welcome.

"This is a surprise." I smiled as I opened the door for her.

"The ladies and I have been doing our homework." She stepped into my office.

"Your what?" I closed the door behind her and offered her my office chair.

"Homework," she repeated. "In human schools, teachers give the students assignments to complete at home based on the material taught in class."

"And I'm the teacher in this scenario?" I clarified.

"Exactly."

"But I didn't give you an assignment."

"We'll call it extra credit, then," she shrugged.

I knew the meaning of both of those words separately, but combined in this context, I had no idea what she meant. "You're just making up words now," I complained.

She rolled her eyes and smiled. Then she noticed the changes I'd made to my office.

"What the hell is that?" She stared at the cot I'd pushed into the back corner of the room. I'd shifted my desk to the right by a few feet to accommodate it.

"It's efficiency at its finest," I retorted.

"I can't tell if that's sad or genius." She stared blankly at the little cot. Since the *Aurora* wouldn't have such a thing on hand, I'd asked for a crew member to find someone to make something.

I suspected he'd found a human for the job, as the pallet wasn't quite long enough for me. My legs hung off the edge of it when I used it, but it was great for short spurts of sleep.

"It's genius." I kind of felt that I was really trying to convince myself instead of her.

"If you say so," she chuckled.

"Now, what's this about the homework?" I sat down on the edge of the cot.

She stared at me for a few moments, then shook her

head. "You look ridiculous. Let's switch seats. Take your chair back. I'll sit on the cot."

I protested. The cot was perfectly suitable.

"You're two feet off the ground!" Vidia laughed.

She was right. I was in more of a squatting position than a sitting position. But still...

"It's comfortable," I insisted.

"Whatever you say." She nodded but clearly didn't believe me, just handed me a datapad showing a map of the area. "We've been figuring out the best way to attack the camps."

"Have you now?" I examined the map. They'd marked out a surprisingly detailed plan of attack for a group of females that had never done something like this before.

"I must say I'm impressed. I'd been thinking along the same lines. I'm sure the strike teams will find this very useful."

"There's something more," Vidia said, her words a trifle hesitant. "I want to have an active part in the air strike. As do Leena and Evie."

Cold ran down my spine and I straightened, as much as I could in this ridiculous position. "Out of the question. None of you have ever received any formal training. It would be a huge liability to involve you."

She cocked an eyebrow. "We're not exactly asking to fly the damn plane. Shuttle. Whatever. Think about it."

"I am. The answer is still no."

It was like she didn't hear me, just rolled on. "You need pilots. And you need as many of your men on the ground as you can spare to fight the Xathi and deal with the cured humans."

"Still no."

She leaned back with a slight grin, obviously enjoying this more than I was. "It's really the only responsible thing for you to do."

"What?"

"By having us go with the pilots, we can deploy the canisters and take notes as to the dispersal patterns and effectiveness without you having to pull more fighters from the ground force."

I shook my head. "Nice try, but still no."

She raised good points, as always, but not enough to get me to agree. My crew understood the nature of combat—the human females didn't.

Even if they were up in the air, high above the camps, something could always go wrong. I wasn't prepared to put more lives at risk than I absolutely had to.

"I'm not going to let this go," she warned, a playful gleam in her eyes.

"Believe me, I know you won't," I teased back.

"Lucky for you, you're off the hook for now. I have other things to discuss with you."

"Off the hook? You humans have the strangest way of speaking." I shook my head.

"It's called an idiom," she laughed. "It means I'm not going to hassle you about letting me and the others go on to the camps."

"Why not just say you're going to stop hassling me?"

"Because that's boring. Humans like to spice things up when they can."

"They like to what?" I laughed at the ridiculousness of her words.

"Make things exciting," she clarified.

"War is exciting. You don't need to use idioms to add excitement when there's war."

"That's a terrible argument," she laughed. I couldn't help but laugh along with her.

This was why I always enjoyed talking to Vidia. Conversations flowed naturally between us like they were second nature.

She could make me laugh, and I couldn't say that about many others.

"What else did you want to discuss?"

"Oh, right. I was going to say something else before you got hung up on idioms. And yes, *hung up* is another idiom. I didn't realize how heavily my language relies on them until I met you and your crew."

"Glad I could help enlighten you," I chuckled. She narrowed her eyes in my direction.

"Anyway," she continued, "there are two things we can't calculate in the lab. We can't calculate how many hybrids there are or how many will be successfully cured. I assume Thribb has calculated how many lifeforms the *Aurora* can support?"

"Many times," I agreed. "Many, many times."

"Do you have any of those calculations? I'd ask Thribb myself, but I don't think he likes me very much."

"I'm not sure Thribb likes me, either," I chuckled dryly. "He continuously sends his calculations to me, but he clears them when variables change and he has to redo them."

"How often do the variables change?" She tilted her head slightly to one side.

"At least twice a day."

"Wow." Her eyes widened. "That seems...excessive."

"It's fun for him." I shrugged. "Or therapy. I assume he's trying to figure out how many the *Aurora* can afford to shelter. Would you like me to ask him to forward the results to you?"

"No." Her brow furrowed. "That's alright. I'm sure he's going to say we're already over capacity or something like that."

"You're probably right." I nodded.

"Is it really the best idea to house the cured people here? They would have just been through a painful and traumatic experience at the hands of aliens. Perhaps they would be more comfortable around other humans."

"That's an excellent point." I rocked back on the cot slightly, thinking. "And I think it's worth mentioning that the med bay on the *Aurora* isn't as extensive as the one on the *Vengeance* when it comes to treating large populations for trauma."

"Isn't it?" That surprised Vidia. "I thought the Urai's technology was more advanced."

"It is. However, this is a starship. All starships have finite resources—whether it's power, beds, supplies, or even space. The *Aurora* med bay is advanced, but it's not designed to be a shelter forever. It can treat the symptoms of extensive physical and mental trauma, but not for a population as large as what we may bring in."

"What happens if one of the crew gets injured?" Her violet eyes widened with concern.

"We aren't completely helpless." I smiled gently. "Dr. Parr and the Urai medic have our backs." Vidia's expression brightened.

"You just used an idiom!"

"I must've picked it up from you," I winked.

I picked up that particular gesture from Axtin, Sakev, and Dax, who often used it with their mates.

Which meant it was probably completely inappropriate for me to use it with Vidia.

Of course it was.

But when her cheeks colored, I couldn't help but feel a small surge of pleasure.

"We keep getting distracted." She looked down at her hands.

"Right. We need to figure out where to put the cured humans." I agreed.

"What do you know about Glymna?"

"A well-fortified and tranquil city like that could be ideal for the recovering humans." I considered the possibilities. "They'd be surrounded by their own kind, too, in a place that, so far, has been left alone by the Xathi."

"Amira suggested using the Gateway for the air strikes. I think we should use them to move the cured people, too."

"Glymna it is," I declared.

"We'll have to appeal to the city, of course," Vidia reminded. "We can't just show up with hundreds of traumatized humans and leave them there."

"Naturally. I'll organize something right away."

"Good."

We fell into silence.

"Was there anything else you needed to discuss?" I asked after a few moments.

"That's all for now." Vidia smiled. She lifted herself from my chair and stepped toward the door. She stopped before opening it and looked back at me over her shoulder. "The girls in the lab said something funny to me earlier."

"Oh?" I was secretly glad she'd found something else to talk about. "What's that?"

"They said I'm the human female version of you, but with twice the energy." I could tell she found the idea amusing.

"I have plenty of energy," I said defensively, though I found the comparison pleasing.

"We both know that's a lie." She looked pointedly at the cot.

"There's nothing wrong with my cot," I laughed.

"How many hours of sleep do you get on that little thing?"

I hesitated before answering. "It's not so much sleeping, as resting my eyes," I admitted. "It's enough."

"Next time I bring you coffee, I'm spiking it with a tranquilizer." Her lips curved in a sweet, teasing smile. *Probably* teasing.

"Now I know not to accept coffee from you."

"I'll find another way," she called over her shoulder as she walked out. "And you'll never see it coming."

VIDIA

I felt like all I'd been doing was running back and forth between the lab and Rouhr's office. Late in the evening after I showed Rouhr the attack plans we'd come up with in the lab, I was on my way back to his office once more.

I'd heard from Leena, who'd been talking to Axtin last night, that a short trip to Glymna was scheduled to appeal to the city leaders.

Which puzzled me.

Rouhr and I had come up with that plan together. I had a hard time believing he'd move forward without me.

He was stepping out of his office when I approached. I almost didn't recognize him. He was wearing a holo-disguise, but the scar on his face was a dead giveaway.

I briefly wondered if he chose not to hide it or if the holo-disguise wasn't capable of camouflaging it.

"I heard some strange news." I placed my hands on my hips, fingers drumming in annoyance that I tried to keep from my tone. The disguise all but confirmed my suspicion.

"What's that?" Rouhr asked. I couldn't tell if he was genuinely oblivious or faking it.

"You're going to Glymna without me."

He took in my tone and posture, finally realizing that I was annoyed. He sighed deeply, as good as an admission.

"Any particular reason why?"

"We're using the Gateway to get there," he said, as if that was a sufficient explanation.

"What's your point?"

"It hasn't been fully tested. Anything could go wrong when we use it."

"Amira and her team used it, and nothing happened to them," I pointed out.

"Which they shouldn't have done. That was too big of a risk."

"But nothing happened to them!"

"That doesn't mean something won't happen to us this time."

"Your logic is flawed. You know that, right?"

He opened his mouth to say something more, but I didn't let him.

"I know the city leaders. I know how to do this kind of negotiation. But you'd rather keep me here out of fear that something *might* happen?"

"Alright," Rouhr said.

"And another thing—wait, what?" I paused.

"Alright. You can come. I know you well enough to know that you're not going to let up. And you're right, I could use your help with the negotiations. I didn't realize you knew the city officials."

"I'm glad you're seeing reason."

I was thrown by how quickly he'd changed his mind. I was prepared for a better argument.

I was almost disappointed, really.

Wearing him down was kind of…fun.

"What was your negotiation plan, anyway?"

"Ask nicely."

"That's a good start." I laughed. "But that's not going to work. City leaders are politicians, not charity workers. If we're going to ask something, we have to be prepared to offer something in return."

"Protection," Rouhr offered.

"Now you're getting it." I grinned. "And another thing, you should lose the holo-disguise."

"What? Why? All of the other towns had vicious

anti-alien groups. I don't think striding in in all of my red and scaly glory is a wise move."

"I can understand how you'd think that at first," I admitted. "But if you show up without the disguise with me by your side, it will send a message of trust and openness, which is something we need right now."

"That makes no sense," Rouhr groaned.

"It's politics! Of course, it doesn't make any sense. It's an intricate dance. I know the steps. You don't. So, a little trust, please?"

"A dance? Was that another idiom?" He cracked a smile. I couldn't help but laugh.

"No, that's a metaphor. You'll figure it all out eventually."

He shut off the disguise, and I followed him down the corridor.

"Besides," I muttered to myself, "I like your red and scaly glory."

Together, we made our way to the ground floor and then to the outside of the ship. I was surprised to see Fen, holding the Gateway in her hands. It amazed me that a little black sphere could open up the whole of space.

"I've asked Fen to come along."

"Oh, so you have no problem dragging her through an experimental rift opening?" I joked.

Rouhr chuckled. "It's not my fault that she's the only who really understands how to use the Gateway."

"I find it hard to believe you didn't have something to do with that, too," I teased. "But it's good that she's coming. I believe we can use the Urai's sonic barriers in the negotiations."

"Ready to head out, General?" My attention snapped to a small team of strike team members, including Axtin and Daxion, standing at attention and armed to the teeth.

"What are they doing?" I asked.

"They're coming, for insurance purposes," Rouhr explained.

"No, they aren't. How is anyone supposed to trust us if you bring in more weaponry than Glymna has in its entire city? They're academics, remember?"

"You can't expect me to go in without backup."

"You're going to send the wrong image," I insisted. "Do you want this to work or not?"

After a long moment of consideration, Rouhr sighed heavily. "I really hope you're not wrong about all this," he muttered to me before addressing his crew. "Change of plans. You're all dismissed."

A murmur of confusion rippled through the assembled team.

"Uh, yes, General." Axtin nodded. The team

dispersed slowly, as if they were expecting to be called back at any moment.

"Go ahead and open a rift, Fen," Rouhr instructed.

Fen nodded and pressed on the sphere. In front of us, a bright white strip of light appeared. It grew wider and wider until I could clearly see the entrance to the city of Glymna on the other side.

Rouhr took my hand in his and lead me to the rift. He stepped through first, then pulled me through once he was sure it was safe.

Fen followed behind and closed the rift when she was through.

"Looks like you were all worked up over nothing." I gave Rouhr a gentle shoulder nudge.

"Is holding hands part of the dance?"

I'd forgotten our hands were still intertwined. "Not the political one." I bit my lip and released him from my grip. I must be more flustered than I thought, saying something like that aloud.

City officials quickly gathered at the main gate of Glymna. Some drew their blasters, while others just stared at the three very different beings approaching their city.

"We mean no harm. I am Vidia Birch, mayor of Fraga. My allies and I seek an audience with your city leaders. They know who I am."

One of the city officials, a captain by the look of his uniform, stepped forward.

"I'll inform them of your arrival at once." He nodded politely. He turned to one of his men. "Keep your blasters on them. If they try anything, shoot them."

I wasn't sure if he meant for me to hear that or not.

"Was this part of your plan?" Rouhr muttered.

"Trust me," I repeated.

Within ten minutes, the three city leaders of Glymna walked out to greet us. The youngest of the three was a woman ten years my senior named Seraphe. She rushed to hug me.

"Vidia, when we heard the news about Fraga, I was so sure you were dead!" she cried. "Why didn't you get in touch sooner?"

"I was helping my friend, General Rouhr, get a shelter for displaced citizens up and running." I tilted my hand towards Rouhr as introduction, not wanting to interrupt Seraphe's flow. "It's been a terribly busy time. Even the Urai, such as our brilliant ally Fen, here," another casual wave, "have been helping"

"Oh, I can imagine!" Seraphe gushed. "I'd expect nothing less of you. Rickon, Vendi, say hello to Vidia!" Seraphe gestured to the two middle-aged men who were looking on. Both men nodded a greeting. I didn't expect anything more, not at this stage of the game.

"As glad as I am to see you all again," I continued,

"we're here to ask a rather large favor. May we go somewhere to talk?"

Seraphe agreed, linking her arm through mine. She and I walked ahead, the others trailed behind us.

"I don't mean to be rude," Seraphe whispered to me, "but you've arrived with some unusual characters."

"I know their appearance is unexpected, but they're both good friends who have proved their desire to help us time and time again. I trust them with my life."

"If you say so." Seraphe shook her head a little.

We drew attention as we walked through the city carved into the mountain. Seraphe led us to a cluster of plush couches under a broad awning in one of the public squares. It's likely she chose the location so there would be plenty of witnesses if something went awry.

Once everyone was seated, I started.

"Time is of the essence, so I'll speak plainly." I explained hybridism, our plan to cure it, and what we needed from Glymna. I tried to leave out as many horrible details as possible. By the time I was finished, the city leaders looked shocked.

"I appreciate your situation," Vendi said carefully, "but we cannot agree to take on an unspecified number of people suffering from a condition we aren't prepared to treat."

Seraphe agreed with Vendi. "And who is to say

assisting you won't draw the Xathi right to our doorstep? They've left us alone so far."

Rickon only grunted in agreement. He wouldn't stop glaring at Rouhr.

"There's a camp of these hybrids not far from your city," Rouhr warned. "It's only a matter of time before they come here."

Seraphe's eyes widened, and she shot worried glances at her two co-leaders.

"I understand that we're asking a lot," I continued. "But we're prepared to make it worth your while. Fen, our Urai friend, has devised a brilliant sonic barrier designed to repel Xathi and hybrids. In addition to teaching you how to identify hybridism and allowing your people unrestricted access to the cure as a precautionary measure, I'm willing to ask Fen and her team to erect a sonic barrier to protect Glymna."

"Oh, well. I still don't know if—" Seraphe started.

I knew this tactic. She was fishing for more.

As sweet as she was, I'd never met a shrewder negotiator.

I cut in before she could say anything else. "Of course, I completely understand." I rose to my feet. "Come, General. We'll have to find another solution."

"Wait!" Seraphe said quickly.

I hid my smile. I'd called her bluff.

"Of course, we're willing to help. I was only saying I

didn't know how many doctors will be available to learn from you on such short notice. But we can provide accommodations while we get everyone organized."

"That would be lovely. You're so kind."

Rouhr looked between me and Seraphe with a slightly bewildered expression, while Seraphe waved over a city official.

"Please escort our guests to the Glymna Center Inn and inform the innkeeper that they are to have three rooms," Seraphe instructed. The official nodded and gestured for us to follow him. "I'll be in touch soon, my dear, with plans and counts. But in the meantime, enjoy yourself!"

I thanked Seraphe, and we went off with the official.

We could have gone back to the *Aurora* through the rift. But staying in Glymna meant we were easily accessible to Seraphe to answer questions, and our continued presence would make it impossible for the situation to be conveniently forgotten or swept aside.

Politics.

The inn the official brought us to was not the nicest in town, but I didn't care. The rooms were small and the innkeeper was gruff, but I was too pleased with my success to be bothered by any of it. As soon as I was installed in my room, I immediately went into Rouhr's.

"See? I told you to trust me." I sang from his doorway.

"You're right." He lifted his hands in surrender. "I apologize for ever doubting you. You're a master at the political dance." He stepped closer to me, so close that I could feel the heat coming off his skin. I looked up at him.

"I guess you learned your lesson, huh?" I tried to joke, but my voice came out too soft.

"Yes." Rouhr said, the smile fading from his lips as his eyes searched mine.

"I'm learning lots of lessons from you, Vidia." His calloused hand gently stroked my cheek, thumb grazing tantalizingly close to my lips.

Then he stepped away, the moment broken.

"I'm looking forward to the next one."

ROUHR

Dreaming about Vidia's silken skin under my hands, I woke up the next morning feeling more refreshed than I had in the past ten years.

That touch at my doorway could have turned into something else, sparked a fire that would have burned for hours... but we both knew it couldn't be an option.

I hadn't planned on touching her, coming so close to kissing her, though I'd be lying if I said I hadn't wanted to for a while now.

But when she came to my doorway, glowing in the wake of her victory, I couldn't resist her.

Neither Fen nor I had been invited to yesterday's discussion. I assume Seraphe and the others had concerns about us that they would've preferred us not to hear.

It didn't bother me, however. They'd need time to get used to having aliens as part of their world, and besides, I'd brought enough reports that needed my attention to last me well into the night.

Once duty was finished, I'd lain awake, mind filled for once with issues other than strategy and tactics.

War and survival.

Vidia filled my thoughts, and I didn't know what to do next.

Once I became a general, I dedicated myself completely to the service. I spent nearly all of my time in space with my crew. I always told myself I'd make time to find a mate later.

The years flew by and before I knew it, I was past my prime and still submerged in battle after battle.

A mate was out of the question for me.

But now, suddenly, somehow, Vidia was in my life.

I didn't know the first thing about courting a mate, not anymore.

Certainly not a human woman.

I pulled on my uniform, and pulled up the next batch of endless reports and requisitions needing my attention.

Duty came first. Duty would always come first.

By the time I'd burned through the reports, the small room had become confining. Summoned or not, I needed to stretch my legs.

At the main level of the inn, the owner sat on a stool behind a small desk. He appeared to be going over his finances. It occurred to me that we were given these rooms free of charge.

This wasn't a large inn. Losing three rooms must have put a damper on his income.

"Excuse me." I stepped up to the desk slowly, not wanting to startle him.

Remarkably, he appeared unfazed by my appearance. He looked at me with the eyes of a man who has seen and done much in his life.

"Hm?" he grunted.

"Have you seen the human woman in my party?" I asked.

"She's in a meeting," he replied.

I thought about tracking Vidia down and joining her. However, I had thought Vidia would've included me if it benefitted the political dance she was orchestrating. If she didn't invite me, I knew she had a good reason.

"I see. What about the other woman?" I asked.

"The blue one with the strange eyes? She went towards the city gates," he explained.

Fen must've started her work on the sonic barrier, as restless at being cooped up as I was.

"Thank you," I said, but hesitated before leaving. I turned back to the innkeeper. "Write up a list of expenses for the rooms and your services. Just because the city leaders are trying to keep me on their good side, it doesn't mean you have to lose money."

The innkeeper looked at me with surprise for a moment before plugging a list of expenses into a datapad. I took the datapad and forwarded the information to the console in my office before handing it back to the innkeeper.

"I'll have it sent to you," I explained. "We appreciate your hospitality." If nothing else, his indifference was preferable to the hostility I'd expected.

The innkeeper simply nodded, and went back to his work as I left.

No one stopped me as I walked through the cavernous city, though the strange looks followed me until I stepped outside the city gates.

Fen was working farther down the slope of the mountain. I jogged down to her.

"Trying to figure out how to set up the barrier?" I asked.

The land was flat and soft where the *Aurora* was docked. It was easy to set up the pikes that harnessed the power of the rift and emitted the sonic frequency. The mountains here were an entirely different matter.

Fen pressed her palm to the speech pad strapped to her hip.

"It will not be easy with so much solid rock," she said. "But for today, I can place a few pikes across the main path leading to the city gates. I believe the mountains have given these humans an advantage over the Xathi."

"I've always known the Xathi to claim their victory by overwhelming their target," I added. "With a single narrow entrance, it'd be far more difficult for the Xathi to do that."

"And the city is almost completely concealed within the mountain. They would be forced to go in blind, and they do not like doing so," Fen concluded.

"I wonder if the Xathi know how much wealth can be found within the city," I mused. "There isn't much in the sense of natural resources, but Glymna has one of the most impressive libraries on the planet."

"The Xathi have never been ones for libraries," Fen replied. She drew a mark in the gravelly slope with her foot, marking where a sonic pike would go. "They prefer to turn lesser species and their innovations into raw materials to fuel their own technology. It's only if they believe a species has superior technology that they will integrate it into their own."

"Did they absorb that from your people?" I asked.

Fen gave me what might be a resentful look.

"Apologies," I said quickly. "I didn't intend to give offense. I'd been at war with the Xathi for a long time, and I still know so little about them. You can imagine how frustrating that is."

Fen's expression softened.

"Of course," she nodded. "The Urai are an ancient race. We've had the time to advance our technology beyond that of many species. We were also aware of the few other races that possessed a similar level of technology. I believe the Xathi incorporated that information from us."

Fen pulled the Gateway from the pack she wore. She opened a small rift.

On the other side, I could see two Urai waiting with sonic pikes. They passed one through the rift to her.

"Let me help," I insisted, offering to take the pike from her.

Fen was stronger than the average human female, but not stronger than a Skotan.

I held the pike with the pointed end directly above the center of the mark Fen had made with her foot. I lifted the pike straight up and slammed it down into the ground. When I released it, it stood straight up on its own.

"Well done," Fen nodded.

We placed four more pikes across the expanse of the pathway leading up to the city gates.

"What next?" I asked.

The pikes around the *Aurora* emitted a faint blue light. The ones we'd just placed were dull.

"I will open a rift to power the sonic pikes," Fen explained.

She first closed the rift she'd used to get the pikes, then she slowly and carefully opened another, much larger, rift high above the city.

"Why does the rift have to be there?" I asked. "Couldn't you draw power from the rift that was already open?"

"A rift that small does not create enough energy to power the sonic pikes," Fen explained. "A large rift opening into deep space can. And, as you know, thousands of energy bursts and cosmic explosions happen in space constantly. That also boosts the energy we can draw from. And it's up so high, so no one down here will be able to get through it by accident."

"But aren't we using the original rift for power right now?" I asked. "Can't that power be harnessed here?"

Fen paused for a moment, as if deciding how to answer in words a non-scientist would understand.

"We harness power from the original rift to provide a steady and stable source of power for the *Aurora*, which is stationary and can be monitored at all times," she said. "But any number of things could go wrong by adding another energy utilization. While conceivable, it is much more efficient for now to use a separate rift, and does not risk interfering with the repairs of the *Aurora*."

I nodded. I could understand the logic behind the thinking. In the heat of battle, simplicity and consistency were far more prized than complex wonders that required many moving pieces.

"Aren't you worried about something coming through it?" I asked.

"It's a larger rift, yes. But not so large that something as big as a Xathi ship could come through. A rift that big would be unstable, just like the one you fell through was, before we were able to harness the power for the *Aurora*."

"I'd still like this rift monitored," I replied. "Even a slim chance of anything coming through is too big of a chance."

"Of course," Fen nodded. "I will alert you of any inconsistencies with this rift."

"Is it possible that, if the *Aurora* were to fly again, we could simply travel through our original rift?" I asked, my mind wandering.

"I would not advise it, General," Fen said promptly. "While it is stable enough to provide power, the stability is borne out of a cautious equilibrium. Traversing the original rift now in a ship would be highly risky."

"What could happen?" I asked.

"At worst case, the rift could close before a ship had completely travelled through it, thereby destroying both the vessel and the rift."

I paused for a moment, lost in that thought. There was something there. I just needed to file it away and ruminate on it later.

We watched the new rift for a few minutes to make sure it was stable.

After I was satisfied, I excused myself to find Vidia. I figured she was finished with her meeting by now. I wanted to check in and see how she was.

And somehow, my morning wasn't complete until I saw her.

I found her in a large conference hall carved entirely from stone deep inside the mountain.

She was speaking to about fifty people. I assumed they were the doctors of Glymna. The city leaders were present as well.

"As I said before," Vidia was saying, "we will provide the cure in the form of a pill for everyone within the city to take as a means of preventive treatment, as well as continuous treatment for those exposed to the airborne form. You all know the known early signs of hybridism, the most common being headaches and patches of scaly skin at the base of the skull. If there are no questions, then I've told you everything you need to know to help your fellow humans."

There was a smattering of polite applause. A handful of doctors approached Vidia before they left, either to compliment her or ask a question.

I stepped up beside her as the crowd eased away.

"Rouhr," she smiled up at me. "I didn't see you come in. How long were you listening?"

"I only just got here." I smiled back. "Fen and I have done what we can for now in terms of defenses. How are things on your end?"

"I think I've given them as much preparation as possible," she shrugged. "There are several rooms like this that are being converted into additional hospital wards. They should be ready by the time we bring people here."

"Excellent," I nodded. "I think we should return to the *Aurora* to prepare the first air strike."

"Cure strike," Vidia corrected.

I gave her a confused look.

"It's what I've started calling them. It's more palatable, less violent, than air strike."

"If that's what you want, it will be called a cure strike."

We walked back through the city gates to rejoin Fen.

"Are we departing?" she asked.

"If you're ready," I replied.

She nodded and used the Gateway to open a rift back to the *Aurora*.

Vidia grabbed my hand before she entered the rift.

"This is so convenient," Vidia marveled as she stepped through. "I'll never want to travel another way."

As we walked back into the *Aurora*, I didn't let go of her hand as we walked back to her cabin.

"The first cure strike will take place tomorrow," I told her. "It's going to be a big day."

She nodded solemnly. "Seraphe and the others will be working through the night, making sure things are prepared on their end."

"It'll be a busy rest of the day for us both," I added, still reluctant to leave her.

She leaned forward, slightly lifting on her toes, face upturned to mine. "You better get some rest when you can."

Cupping her cheek, I stooped down, brushing my lips over hers, the burst of sweetness sparking my blood.

"You, too."

VIDIA

"Are you sure you can convince them?" Evie asked as we hurried through the corridors to get to the docking bay before the cure strike team was ready to leave.

Leena blazed a trail ahead of us. No one wanted to get in her way when she had that look of determination on her face.

"I've already talked to Rouhr about it once," I explained. "He knows how I feel, and I warned him that I'm going to bring it up again. I think telling him your concerns will win him over."

I still wanted to participate in the cure strikes, as did Evie and Leena. Jeneva and Mariella were just fine with staying on the ground, while Amira preferred to work with Fen and the Gateway.

I hadn't stopped thinking about Rouhr since he'd walked me to my cabin. When he touched me in Glymna I was surprised, but also, somehow, not surprised. When he kissed me, it'd felt like coming home.

As natural as every other part of our relationship, like something that was always supposed to happen.

But still a spice, the element of the unknown. All adding up to a puzzle I wanted to solve.

For the first time since the Xathi arrived, I wished there was less work to be done. I wanted to spend more time with Rouhr outside work, to see if there really was something there.

It took great effort to put those thoughts aside for the time being. I couldn't forget about matters at hand just because I'd acknowledged that I had a crush.

I was a grown woman. I should be beyond crushes. And yet, here I was.

"Looks like they're getting ready to take off." I pointed to the far end of the docking bay where the strike teams gathered. I couldn't see Rouhr from where I was, but I was sure he was there.

"Come to see us off, ladies?" Rouhr asked when we approached the strike teams. I paused, caught off guard by his choice of words.

"What do you mean 'us'?"

I looked him over. He was fully suited up in tactical gear and armed to the teeth.

"I've sat in my office for too long. I'd rather be out with my crew, making a difference."

I smiled, though I couldn't help but feel worried.

"That's very admirable of you," I said. "But we didn't come just to wish you luck."

"I knew it." Rouhr gave me a sly grin. "You still want to go up in one of the air units. I almost believed you weren't going to bring it up again."

"You know me better than that." I smirked. "But this time, it's not just about me wanting things to go my own way. Evie has some concerns you should be aware of before you decide who's going up in the air units."

I nodded to Evie, so she could take it from here.

"I know an airborne cure sounds simple enough," she started. I could tell she was still intimidated by Rouhr, despite how patiently he listened. "But there's a lot more to it than pulling the tab and throwing it out of an air transport."

"My crew is very good at following directions," Rouhr said kindly.

"I'm sure they are," Evie replied. "But I've seen their field notes. Leena and I are going to need to know exactly how the gas disperses, how quickly it settles, what adjustments need to be made to the cannisters." She raised her chin. "I don't think they're able to take the notes we'll need in a format we'll be able to use, in order to optimize for the next strike."

Rouhr hesitated, while I tried to hold back my smile.

"I'm sure you can give them a sufficient overview."

I could hear the doubt in his voice.

"Not if you want to complete the first cure strike today," Evie told him. She swallowed hard. "And I know you've got a schedule you want to keep."

Rouhr considered his options for a few moments before letting out a sigh of defeat. "Very well."

"You're making the right decision." I rested my hand on his shoulder. "This is the greatest medical discovery of Evie's career. She deserves to be there to see if it works."

"That's true," Rouhr admitted, but I could tell he still wasn't happy with the idea.

"Besides," I added as worry gnawed at my stomach, "with the three of us up in the air, more of your crew will be on the ground to watch your back."

"You're worried about me?" Rouhr laughed. "I've been doing this for a very long time, Vidia." He tilted my chin up to meet my eyes. "You have nothing to worry about."

"I only worry because I care." I shrugged, looking away. Whatever this was between us, it couldn't be now. Couldn't be here.

Except it was.

"So do I," his voice was soft. "That's one of the reasons I was so against you going up in the air units. Also, you're incapable of taking orders."

"I like that you care so much." I smiled, ignoring that last bit. "Not just about me but about everyone. I think that's what makes you a great general."

"Others would beg to differ."

"Others are stupid." I tossed my head for dramatic effect to make him laugh. It worked.

"Come on," he urged. "If you insist on being part of dangerous missions, let's get you some gear, and I'll need to make a few reassignments."

Since I was going to be in an air unit, out of combat range, I only needed a comm to stay in contact with Evie, Leena, and the ground teams. I also took a pair of vision goggles to see better from a distance. Evie and Leena were given the same.

Rouhr walked me over to a small transport unit. It was sleek and streamlined, built for speed and agility. There was a seat for the pilot and another single seat behind it.

"D'val will be your pilot." Rouhr gestured to a tall K'ver with a serious expression. He then turned to speak to him.

"You are to keep her as far from the line of fire as possible. Once you reach the camp, deploy the cure and observe its effects from a distance. Once the ground teams receive the signal to move in, you are to return here."

"What?" I blurted. "But what if something happens?"

Rouhr turned his attention back to me.

"You're going to be kept out of harm's way whether you like it or not." His voice was stern, a determined gleam in his eyes.

"Fine," I grumbled.

Rouhr only laughed as he walked back to join the ground teams.

As soon as he was out of earshot, I leaned toward D'val, the pilot. "What are my chances of getting you to disregard his orders?"

"Your dedication is admirable. But I'm not disobeying the general."

"Well, at least I tried." I shrugged.

"Why are you so determined to go against him?" D'val asked as he performed his final external checks on the unit. There was no aggression in his voice, just genuine curiosity.

"It's not that I wish to go against Rouhr. But when I feel like I could be of more help, I don't like being stopped."

D'val laughed.

"I think that's something all of us can relate to. I'm not happy about leaving my general on the ground, either. But he knows what he's doing. He's proved that time and time again."

"Then why do I have to constantly cajole him into the smartest option?"

D'val took my hand to help me into the back seat before climbing in himself.

"You realize no one else is able to make him change his mind, right? I think he has a soft spot for you. But that's none of my business." He focused on his controls. "You should test your comm before we head out."

I fiddled with the switches until I was able to hear the others.

"Can you hear me, Evie?"

"Yes," Evie replied. "Can you hear me, Leena?"

"Affirmative," Leena chirped.

"I think we're all set," I said to D'val.

He nodded and fired up the air unit. We lifted off the deck and flew out of the docking bay.

I could see the craft carrying Leena and Evie on either side of me. I peered over the side. Below, Fen and Amira worked to open a rift for us to pass through.

I'd already lost sight of Rouhr.

I knew he was capable in combat, but the thought of him directly in harm's way, like he would soon be, made me uneasy. Maybe this was what he felt every time I tried to get involved.

A light flashing on my comm captured my attention. I pressed the corresponding button.

"Vidia, do you read me?" Rouhr's warm voice wrapped around me.

"Yes."

"Good. Be safe. I'll meet up with you as soon as I can."

I couldn't help but smile. "You're the one who needs to be safe."

He laughed, and we clicked back to the main comm line.

D'val steered us through the rift. I looked down at the hybrid camp.

Camp wasn't the right term to describe what I saw. There were no shelters, no fires…nothing one would expect to see. There was only a large round pen filled with hybrids, surrounded by Xathi guards as they circled, their unceasing jerky movements catching at my heart.

The Xathi shrieked when they spotted us, the hybrids began to howl. I clutched one of the pressurized canisters in my hand, waiting for Evie's signal.

D'val lowered us slowly until we were even with Evie's unit. Leena's unit followed suit.

"Pull the tab and drop them as straight as you can," Evie reminded us.

I pulled the tab on the canister and dropped it through the chute of the air unit.

A faint trail of pink vapor marked its journey down. I saw Evie and Leena's canisters falling, too. When they hit the ground, billowing clouds of pink vapor were released.

I put on my vision goggles and adjusted them until I could get a better view.

"Can anyone see anything?" I asked into the comm.

"Yes, the hybrids are responding!" Evie shrieked with excitement. "Start recording, notate everything you can see!"

"Try to get a better viewpoint," I urged D'val. He slowly shifted the transport unit until I was able to see more.

Soon, a percentage of the hybrids no longer acted rabid. More and more stood still, holding their heads and looking confused.

The crystal formations on their bodies were slowly changing, too. It was like they were being drained of color and energy, like the queen's influence was being forced out of their bodies.

"Call in the ground teams!" Evie instructed.

I switched back to Rouhr's frequency.

"It's working!"

"We're going in. I'll see you soon."

His end of the line went silent, and I held my breath.

ROUHR

As my team and I moved toward the camp, I kept an eye on the sky to make sure the air units returned to the *Aurora*. Two of them did almost immediately, but one lingered. I was certain it was Vidia, trying to watch as much as she could before D'val turned around.

I didn't have to tune into the comm to imagine her negotiating with him, pleading with him to stay, so she could keep an eye on everything.

There was a reason why I assigned D'val to be her pilot. He was more stubborn than she was, and loyal to a fault.

Vidia would never be able to sway him from my orders.

But she'd try.

Sure enough, eventually the lingering air unit turned around and disappeared, the rift closing behind them.

The Xathi hadn't noticed us yet. Their attention was focused on the pink vapor clouds and the hybrids.

One of the hybrids standing close to the edge of the pen ran its hands up and down its sides, like it was confused by its own body. It clawed at the crystal coating until a chunk broke loose. From where I stood, I could see a sliver of pale human skin.

It was only a matter of time before the Xathi figured out what the pink smoke was doing to their captives.

As soon as they did, I knew slaughter would start.

"Tu'ver, get the Xathi's attention," I instructed.

Tu'ver lifted his sniper rifle and shot the nearest Xathi clean through one of its leg joints. It shrieked and stumbled. The others scuttled over to it.

Tu'ver fired again, purposefully missing the vulnerable leg joints and striking a Xathi right between the eyes.

It spotted us in the instant before it died, and now all of them knew we were here.

There were ten in total, all Hunters. They shoved through the dazed hybrids and scrambled over the pen fence to get to us.

Those on my team who excelled in hand-to-hand combat dove at them.

I moved carefully, waiting until a distracted Xathi gave me the perfect chance to shoot out his legs.

One of the Xathi spun, flinging its rock-solid body in my direction.

I dodged, but not fast enough. The impact temporarily knocked the breath out of me.

I recovered quickly, but I suppose sitting at a desk for so long had made me a bit rusty.

Vidia would never let me hear the end of this.

Skrell.

I was still flat on my back when the Xathi leaped at me once more. I activated the blade attachment of my blaster and shoved it through the weak spot where the Xathi's head met its body. It shrieked and writhed as I pushed the blade deeper.

Some of my team took advantage of its immobilized state and took out its legs, then Axtin delivered the fatal blow to its head with his hammer.

Once I found my rhythm again, the Xathi were no match for us. It was strange to admit, but being back on the battlefield felt good.

Great, even. It'd been too long.

It took us less than ten minutes to cut down the Xathi.

I was sure the Xathi queen had been watching us through the eyes of her now-deceased minions.

She'd send more guards to the remaining camps.

We'd have to prepare accordingly; today's easy victory wouldn't be repeated.

But for now, I'd take it.

Most of the pink smoke had dissipated. I made a mental note of the time, sure that Leena and Evie would want the information.

The humans closest to where the canisters had dropped looked the most normal. I could see that most of them had already undergone some degree of physical change. The ground inside the pen was littered with discarded chunks of crystal.

A shriek got my attention. A group of humans that still looked entirely hybrid were circling a cluster of humans that could barely stand, let alone defend themselves.

"Get in there," I ordered my team.

We leaped over the fence.

I launched a chunk of discarded crystal at the unaffected hybrids. One of them dashed for me. I subdued it and pinned it to the ground with my weapon across its neck.

"Can you hear me?" I demanded as it thrashed beneath me. "Do you understand me?"

It only continued to shriek and writhe. I looked into its eyes. There was nothing left of the human it once was.

With a heavy sigh, I reached forward and snapped its neck as quickly as I could.

Skrell and twice skrell. This would be the part of the report I didn't want to share with the women. I didn't want to see the brightness of Vidia's eyes dim.

But she deserved the truth. They all did.

After examining the dead hybrid, it was easy to differentiate it from the humans susceptible to the curse. The hybrid crystal formations were still bright. Not glowing, exactly, but alive somehow.

On the other hand, the crystals that covered the humans were dull, almost gray in color, and crumbling. I didn't expect it to take long for the humans to be free of their crystal shells once they were in Glymna.

"I'm sorry we couldn't do more for you," I whispered and got to my feet. "Some are too far gone for the cure to work," I announced. "Find them and keep them away from the recovering humans."

As my team set to work on accomplishing the task, I looked around the pen. Hundreds of humans had been kept here for who knew how long.

I didn't know if hybrids had to eat, but humans certainly did. Their bodies were weak. Many of them had sunk to the ground.

I approached several bodies, thinking they were dead, but they were just in a deep sleep.

Those who were still awake watched me with wary gazes. I was glad we'd worn holo-disguises. I don't know how the humans would've reacted to our natural forms.

I wished Vidia was here. She'd know exactly how to comfort them.

"You have nothing to fear now," I spoke loudly and clearly.

Some of the humans flinched at the sound of my voice. I lowered my voice before I continued speaking. "We're here to help. There's nothing to be afraid of now."

Those nearest to me nodded. I hoped they understood.

My attention was pulled from the humans when Sakev jogged up to me.

"We've neutralized the last of the unaffected hybrids."

"How many were there?" I asked.

"Only about thirty or so. Not a bad percentage when it's all considered."

By my estimation, there were at least five hundred people in the pen. No, thirty wasn't bad at all. I bet Dr. Parr would be thrilled by her cure's success rate.

"We need to get these people out of here." I sighed. "They need food, water, and shelter."

"We'll work on getting those who can walk up and moving." Sakev nodded before jogging off again.

I picked up my comm.

"Fen, open a rift to Glymna."

"Yes, General."

Within seconds, a shimmering portal of light appeared before us. Many of the humans backed away, covering their sensitive eyes.

"It's all right everyone!" I announced. "It's perfectly safe. This will take you to Glymna, where you will be able to recover in peace and safety."

Still, none of the humans moved, even though the gates of Glymna were visible on the other side of the rift. There were people, including the city leaders, on the other side, as well.

I wracked my brain for anything that would help convince the humans to trust me.

"Vrehx." I waved him over. "Go through with Dax and Tu'ver and tell the city officials that we have about five hundred newly cured humans who need immediate attention."

The trio stepped through the rift. As I'd hoped, many of the newly cured humans saw them walk through and come out on the other side unharmed.

One young human male, less starved-looking than the rest, stepped forward and examined the rift. He looked back at the others once before stepping through.

I released the breath I hadn't realized I was holding.

Emboldened by the first human, others approached

the rift and walked through. My crew and I helped those who couldn't go through on their own. It took some time, but eventually, we got everyone out of the pen and into the safety of Glymna.

The first cure strike was a success.

VIDIA

I paced the length of the docking bay, waiting for news.

"Vidia." I didn't realize Evie had walked over to me. She grabbed my shoulders, effectively stopping me from pacing any further. "You need to relax."

"How can I, when I don't know what's happening?"

"We'll know soon."

"It's taken too long," I said. "Something must have gone wrong."

"Or Rouhr has his hands full with several hundred traumatized humans," Evie soothed. "Goodness, I can't believe how on edge you are."

"I can't believe how on edge you *aren't*."

"I'm not on edge because I know we did our part

well, and I trust the ground team to do their part well, too," Evie explained.

"Rouhr hasn't been out in the field in a while." That stupid, gnawing tightness in my belly wouldn't let go.

"You're worrying about him more than I'm worrying about my own partner." Evie laughed. "Have a little faith in him. There's a reason he's the general."

I did have faith in him, though.

More than I'd ever had faith in anyone else.

At that moment, the comm I was still wearing crackled to life.

"Civilians have been escorted to Glymna," Rouhr said in an official-sounding voice.

I looked at the comm. I was still on the main channel, not a private one.

"All the Xathi and remaining hybrids have been dealt with." Before I could say anything, Rouhr clicked off.

"Did you hear that?" I asked Evie.

"No, I gave my comm back."

"They're in Glymna now."

"Why don't you sound happier about that?" Evie looked at me, one eyebrow raised.

"Because there are hundreds of traumatized people that need our help. I think we should get the cure pills."

"Already packaged them up ahead of time." Evie

grinned. "And for the record, I think you're tremendously happy that Rouhr's okay, and you're just too scared to show it."

"What's there to be scared of?" I rolled my eyes.

"Exactly." Evie playfully poked my arm. "I'll grab Leena if you want to get Fen to open a rift."

I nodded, and Evie hurried away.

As I searched for Fen, I thought about what Evie had said. As ridiculous as it sounded, she might have had a point.

I was afraid for Rouhr while he was rescuing the cured people. That was reasonable. They were traumatized, there were so many variables anything could have happened.

But what I didn't tell Evie was that the relief of knowing he was okay, the wonderful feeling that bloomed through my entire body, sparked a different sort of fear. An illogical one.

I found Fen nearby, discussing the mechanics of the Gateway with Amira.

"Sorry to interrupt. But could you open a rift to Glymna? Rouhr's just brought the newly cured there."

"Of course." Fen nodded.

"Can I do it this time?" Amira asked with a hopeful expression.

Fen considered for a moment before nodding and

passing the Gateway to Amira. She took a moment to marvel at the black sphere before pressing methodically on its surface.

"Leena and Evie will be coming along shortly," I explained to Fen before stepping through the rift.

I found myself in the middle of the main city square. It was so crowded, I could barely move. The people around me were horrified by my sudden appearance.

"I'm so sorry," I apologized to everyone at once. It was then that I took in their appearance.

They were all far too pale. Their eyes were slightly glazed, as if they were coming out of a trance, and they were all very thin.

These were the survivors.

"Don't worry," I said quickly. "I'm here to help."

"Vidia," one said in a raspy voice.

"Hannah?" I stepped closer to the girl who was the daughter of one of my secretaries.

She nodded and I opened my arms to embrace her, letting her decide if she wanted to be touched or not.

She walked into my arms and rested her cheek against my shoulder. I held her lightly. Her body was so weakened, I didn't want to hurt her.

"Come with me," I urged her when we broke apart. "Let's see if we can bring some organization to this chaos."

I winked at her, hoping her spark was still there. She managed to smile back and I let go of a breath I hadn't realized I was holding.

Together, we wove carefully through the crowd.

I was alarmed by how quiet it was. Most of the survivors stood in silence, waiting to be told what to do. I imagined most of them were in some form of shock.

Hannah and I made it to the center of the square, where city officials had set up a few tables. Rouhr was standing beside one of the tables, still wearing his holo-disguise and scrolling through a datapad with a confused look on his face.

"Rouhr!" I called out. His head snapped up and a smile spread across his face.

"I'm glad you're here. I have no idea where to start. Who's this?" He smiled at Hannah.

"This is Hannah. I knew her mother before all of this happened."

Hannah nodded a greeting.

"I'm glad you're with us, Hannah," Rouhr said.

My heart did a little flutter every time he spoke. Dammit.

"Have the doctors started their examinations?"

"I have no idea. I can't find anyone, and no one knows who I am." He gestured to his disguised skin.

"Right." I sighed. "Hannah? Do you think you can stay with my friend while I sort this out?"

Hannah nodded and took a step closer to Rouhr while I dove back into the crowd.

On the far side of the square, the doctors were gathered, looking as overwhelmed as Rouhr had.

"What's the holdup?" I demanded.

"We…just don't know where to begin," the doctor closest to me said. "We've never really worked with trauma of this scale."

Seriously? I bit back my words, and dug in.

With a disaster, the first thing was to get started. It usually didn't matter where, just get started.

"Hello," I said in a gentle voice to the nearest survivor. The man looked at me with wary eyes. "Would you like some help?"

"Medicine," was all he said.

"The doctors have more of the medicine that made you better," I explained. "Come with me, and they'll help you."

The man stepped closer to me, and I handed him to the doctor.

Spacing the rest of the physicians in a line, I repeated the process until the survivors started to form lines of their own accord, then the doctors broke out of their analysis paralysis and began examinations.

I gestured to one of the doctors. "There you go.

You've begun. The cure pills have been sent ahead by our team on the *Aurora*. Give everyone a single pill and monitor them closely. Dr. Parr and Dr. Dewitt will want to see your notes. When you've examined and treated them, send them to the center of the square. I'll be there."

The doctors nodded and got to work.

I made my way back to the tables at the center. On one of the tables was a map showing the areas that had been set up to take in the survivors.

"Rouhr." I waved him over. "Comm your crew and tell them to start urging people towards the doctors on the west side of the square. Try to keep them in line, if possible."

Rouhr nodded and sent a message through his comm.

"When the people are sent back here, we'll try to record their information. If they can't remember, we will send them to the shelters north of the square, so we can ask them later. If they can remember, we'll send them to the shelters to the east. I'm going to tell the plan to the volunteers."

The volunteers looked terrified. They weren't expecting anything like this when they signed on to help.

Small, easy-to-repeat steps.

One ran to get two spools of colored cord, so that

every volunteer would know which set of shelters each person should be directed to.

Half of the rest hurried to the tables to take names, start the tracking. The remainder stationed themselves where they could direct each group in the appropriate direction.

When I returned to Rouhr's side, he looked thoroughly impressed.

"You make it look so easy," he laughed. "It's a different sort of battlefield, I suppose."

"Years of practice," I shrugged, though his praise lit a warm glow in my chest. "Let's get Hannah in to see one of the doctors."

I accompanied Hannah to a doctor and told her I'd be at the tables when she was done. She looked much less afraid than she had before.

"How long have you been doing things like this?" Rouhr gestured broadly to the square as we made our way back to the central tables.

I thought about it for a moment before speaking.

"My whole life, I suppose. My parents died when I was very young. I had no other family in Fraga or anywhere that I knew of, and I sure as hell didn't want to get put into the city's program for orphans. I spent most of my younger years doing odd jobs for food and shelter. Everyone in the poorer areas of Fraga knew who I was, became my family in a way.

Despite my parents' deaths, I still had a fairly good childhood."

"I'm so sorry about your parents." The genuine sympathy in his eyes made my heart flutter again.

"It's okay," I assured him. "As I grew older, I noticed more and more shady things about the city. As a little street rat, no one outside of the poor areas paid much attention to me. That worked to my advantage. I learned all Fraga's secrets, how greedy and corrupt the city leaders were. One day, I realized the only way to defeat them was to beat them at their own game. I was elected mayor when I was twenty-seven. The youngest to ever be elected, all because the people in the poorer communities unanimously voted for me."

"That's incredible," Rouhr said.

"It wasn't all sunshine and roses. I had to make some difficult choices. Corruption takes a long time to undo. I don't think it ever goes away completely once it's been able to rot the insides of a city. But I was able to make positive changes. Everyone saw that, even the people who didn't want me as mayor. We were on our way to becoming a truly united city until the Xathi attacked."

"Oh." Rouhr's smile faded, his jaw tight. "From where I'm standing, it looks like you've managed to keep doing good despite the Xathi."

"I try my best." I shrugged. "I don't think it'll ever be enough."

"It's more than enough." Rouhr rested a hand on my shoulder. I let myself lean into him.

We stayed like that for a while, an island of peace within the cacophony of war.

A war that had brought us together.

But what was I going to do about it?

ROUHR

Within a few hours, Glymna's square was the picture of efficiency. Vidia worked tirelessly, moving from one task to the next without breaking her stride. I didn't work side by side with her the entire time, but I tried to stay close to her as much as I could.

I'd been working with her in a professional manner for some time now. But as I worked alongside her here, I got to see more of Vidia, beyond the driven woman I already knew. She had a remarkable capacity for patience, kindness, and compassion.

When survivors became distressed when they couldn't remember their names. or where they were from, she knew exactly how to soothe them.

As a general, I thought I was overly familiar with

every aspect of war. I knew the destruction it brought all too well.

But this was a transition I'd never been present for. The slow progress from destruction to rebirth.

I was proud to have a hand in it.

Most of my men appeared to be enjoying themselves, as well. A few of them were helping the Glymna volunteers take names, but most of them were simply talking to the survivors.

I felt a sense of fatherly pride when I looked at them. They'd all come a long way. As strange as humans were, they were having a profound effect on my crew.

Now I had to return to the *Aurora*. There were reports to fill out and preparations for the next cure strike to make.

Vidia needed to stay in Glymna for a little while longer, and while I was hesitant to leave her, she insisted.

She was right, of course.

But I still made sure she had a comm.

A few of the crew asked to stay, to continue to assist with the resettlement efforts. I allowed everyone who wanted to stay and wasn't needed for preparations for the next strike to stay behind.

"Fen," I called through the comm.

"Yes, General?" she replied.

"We're going back to the *Aurora* now," I said. "Some

are staying behind and will come through another rift later."

"Noted," Fen said.

A few moments later, a rift opened before me. My crew and I strode into the main common area of the *Aurora*, near my office. Fen was becoming remarkably good at directing rifts.

"Thank you, Fen," I said into the comm.

"You're welcome, General," she replied before clicking her comm off.

"I have fantastic news." Thribb appeared at my side.

I didn't even hear him coming. He was getting too good at that.

"More fantastic than saving over five hundred lives?" I asked.

"What?" He blinked twice before his eyes widened with realization. "Oh! The humans. No, not quite as fantastic as saving all of those lives, but close."

"What is it?" I asked.

I couldn't remember the last time Thribb had been so excited about something.

The idea shouldn't have filled me with dread, but it did.

"The hull will be fully sealed by sundown, and the engines, thrusters, and onboard environmental systems are almost fully repaired!" Thribb was practically giddy.

It was unsettling. He was talking louder than he usually did. I could tell my crew had overheard.

Most continued about their duties, cleaning and returning their gear and filling out today's reports. Others, however, paused. They were clearly listening, waiting to see what other valuable bits of information Thribb would drop.

"How is that possible?" I asked. "Repairs on the internal systems weren't meant to start until after the hull was finished. That was your recommendation, at least."

I specifically remembered Thribb compiling a list of repairs in order of highest priority to lowest. One repair couldn't start until the previous one was completed and the remaining resources were recalculated.

"The engines and thrusters have an automated self-repairing system that started working the moment power was restored to the *Aurora*," Thribb said excitedly.

"Is that so?" My brow furrowed. "Why hasn't this been mentioned until now?"

"I wasn't sure it would actually repair anything," Thribb explained quickly. "I didn't want to get anyone's hopes up in case it didn't work properly."

"How convenient," I replied.

"Isn't it?" Thribb sounded so pleased. "Assuming

everything goes as I want it to, I can run tests on the *Aurora's* systems this evening. We could leave tomorrow if everything goes well!"

This was...interesting.

I wasn't an engineer, but I'd served on enough ships to know that it took longer than a few hours to test the systems necessary for space travel. That was true, even if the ship wasn't being repaired after a crash.

On an alien planet.

With minimal repair facilities.

"Don't you think you're being a bit premature?" An engineer that didn't want to hedge his bets, talk about variables, made me nervous.

"We can finish the tests quickly enough," Thribb insisted. "There's no reason for further delay."

The crew members weren't even trying to hide their interest now. "Is that true, General?" Karzin asked. "We could leave tomorrow?"

"I don't know," I replied. "I've never heard of these automated repair systems until now. Naturally, I'll have to discuss it with the Urai. I can't simply take Thribb's word that they're safe."

"But if they are safe, we're leaving, right?" Rokul's voice was calm, but the fiery look in his eyes didn't escape my notice.

"We've already had this conversation." Keeping my voice down and my temper under control was a struggle. "Am I hearing that some of my crew are willing to leave a job half done?"

"It's not our job anymore," Rokul shrugged.

My temper flared. Before Rokul or any of the other crew members could react, I grabbed his arm, pulled him to me, and twisted his arm around behind his back.

When Rokul struggled, I pushed the toe of my boot into the back of his knee, forcing it to buckle. Once he was on the deck, I put my knee between his shoulder blades and tightened my grip on his arm. At least he was smart enough to stop fighting me.

The others looked on in shock. They'd never seen me do anything like this before. It wasn't the sort of leader I wanted to be, but that didn't mean I wasn't capable when it was necessary.

And it was necessary.

"Listen now, and listen well," I snarled. "I have given all of you a mission. We are not leaving until that mission is completed. If you disagree with that, I will walk you off the *Aurora* myself, and we will see how long it takes you to leave this planet from there. Do you want me to do that?"

"No," Rokul grunted from underneath me.

"I didn't hear you," I shot back.

"No, Sir!" he yelled.

I released his arm and lifted my knee off his back. I extended a hand to help him to his feet. He took it.

"All of you are to go down to the galley and report to Snipes," I said. "He is your superior for the next week. When this week is up, I better receive glowing reports from him, or else there will be another week. And another. And another. As many as it takes for each and every one of you to prove to me that you deserve the rank you were given."

They stood rigid, mouths agape.

"Did I mumble?" I demanded. "Report to Snipes, *now!*"

The crew members hurried off, tripping over each other as they went.

Thribb stood off to the side, looking nervous.

"I'm tempted to send you down to Snipes, as well," I grumbled.

I disliked losing my temper.

"I—" Thribb stammered.

"If I didn't know any better, I'd say you chose that moment to announce these surprise repairs for the sole purpose of riling the crew." I looked at him through narrowed eyes.

"You can't be serious," Thribb scoffed, though a hint of nerves threaded through his voice. "I discovered what I thought was good news and reported to you immediately."

Thribb held my gaze, thin lips pursed.

Afraid, or just angry?

Anxious for his work, to return to the war, or was there something else in there?

I sighed. "In the future, you will make your reports to me in appropriate, calmer fashion. You're dismissed."

"General," Thribb nodded before walking away.

I couldn't remember the last time I felt so tired.

VIDIA

It had been a few hours since Rouhr and his crew returned to the *Aurora*. I'd been working non-stop since then, yet there was still so much to be done.

The doctors were still seeing survivors. The main square was still filled with dazed people waiting to be examined and then given a bed.

The rooms we were using for shelters were spacious. Hundreds of cots had been found, built, and donated. Rows upon rows of these cots filled the rooms allocated to the survivors.

Any doctor that was not currently giving examinations was stationed in these rooms, watching over the patients. Most of the survivors crawled into bed and went to sleep as soon as they were given a cot.

"Everyone is so tired," I mused to Hannah.

She was comfortable in her human body once more and much more talkative than she'd been earlier, insisting on staying with me as I worked.

At first, I worried about her health. I wanted her to rest, but she didn't want to. I kept a close eye on her, all the same. The moment she started to look unwell, I would march her right back to her cot.

"We didn't sleep," she explained. "None of us were allowed to. I don't think the queen knew what sleep was."

"The Xathi don't sleep?" I asked.

"Not the ones I saw," Hannah replied.

We walked together through the rows of cots, the set-up perfect for medical emergencies. The doctors on watch duty could be notified almost immediately if needed.

However, with no dividers and roughly seventy people per room, they offered nothing in the way of privacy.

Despite all of the people that had flooded into the city, there were still cots to spare. But I didn't think there were enough to simultaneously fit the survivors from all three camps. I had to find a place for the people from the first camp to make room for people coming in from the final two camps.

I racked my brain for a solution as Hannah and I walked together through the wards, back to the city square, past massive homes carved into the stone itself.

"I've got it!" I exclaimed suddenly, startling Hannah in the process. "Let's make a broadcast and ask people to open up their homes to the survivors that just need rest, not further medical attention."

"That could work," Hannah nodded.

"We'll keep it simple, just a written message that will show up on the public screens," I continued.

"You could use my picture, if you want," Hannah offered.

"Are you sure?" With my hand on her shoulder, I could feel her small bones under my fingers. How much more could she take?

"I think it'll make people more likely to help," she answered, biting her lip.

"You have a big heart, Hannah. Your mother would be proud."

For the first time since she was rescued, she smiled.

We found the central broadcasting station for the city. After taking one look at Hannah, they couldn't deny our request.

Within twenty minutes, Hannah's picture ran along the bottom of every broadcast screen in the city with the message reading *'Help me reclaim my life'* and where to go to offer help.

"Good job, Hannah."

By the time we returned to the city square, three people had offered their homes.

I caught Hannah yawning and sent her back to her cot to sleep.

I gave instructions to the doctors to send anyone who seemed ready to leave immediate medical supervision to the central desk to be matched with a generous resident.

Every nerve in my body felt alive and wired. I'd missed this level of productivity.

There was still so much to do, it was probably better if I stayed here in Glymna for the night.

I'd let Rouhr know as soon as I reported back to Evie on how well her and Leena's cure was working.

I didn't think Evie had a comm on her at the moment, so I borrowed a comm unit to call her lab. There was a good chance she was still working. I found a quiet alcove and waited for her to pick up.

"Yes?" she answered in a brisk tone. Definitely still working.

"It's me," I announced.

"How's the cure working?" she asked.

"Fantastically," I replied. "There's almost no side effects. How did you manage that?"

"What do you mean by almost?" Evie asked, ignoring my compliment.

"A few people are having allergic reactions," I

explained. "Something in the cure is making their skin red and blotchy, but it goes away with antihistamines."

"Interesting," Evie hummed. "But nothing serious, right? No swelling, no difficulty breathing?"

"Nothing like that," I said.

"That's good," she said. "Out of all the side effects that could occur, that's one of the mildest. Anything else I should know?"

"About one third of all the people we've rescued are experiencing memory loss," I explained. "I think that's the Xathi's fault, not yours."

"I'd like to do brain scans on those affected."

"I'll let the doctors know," I agreed.

"No one has reverted back, right?" I could hear the worry in her voice.

"Nope," I said proudly. "As far as we can tell, the queen has been kicked out of their brains for good. The doctors have given everyone instructions on how to fight her off the way you did, just in case, though."

"Tell the doctors to examine every patient daily to check for scaly patches of skin and bumps on the base of their skulls, that's the earliest sign," Evie instructed.

"They already know," I reassured her. "Don't worry. Things are going better than I'd ever hoped they would."

"I'll stop worrying when the Xathi are all dead and gone," Evie muttered.

"Same here," I sighed. "Anything happening on the *Aurora* I should know about?"

"We're almost done making a slightly stronger batch of the airborne cure. Jeneva found an animal extract that makes the pink mist dissipate more slowly. Longer exposure might help the ones the cure didn't work on the first time around."

"Sounds like it's worth a shot," I agreed.

"Also, Sakev and I think it's worth going around to the smaller towns that haven't been bothered as much by the Xathi," she continued. "We can hand out the pills and construct sonic barriers. If we do it right, we could have little safe havens for people to live."

"That's perfect!" I gasped. "Maybe I have some survivors here that are from those towns. It would be great to send them back to their original homes."

"I bet that would speed up their recovery, too," Evie agreed.

"I'll talk to the doctors about that," I said. "I need to comm Rouhr, and let him know I'll be staying here overnight."

"Oh!" Evie exclaimed before I could say goodbye. "Sakev told me there was an interesting moment with Rouhr and a few of his men right after they got back from Glymna."

"What happened?" I asked, dread pooling.

"Thribb and some of the strike team members tried

to urge Rouhr to leave Ankau before curing the other camps," Evie explained, voice heavy. "Thribb's been running repairs in secret, or something like that. The *Aurora* is almost completely fixed up."

"That little sneak," I muttered. "Why is he so against us? I don't understand."

"I don't think it's that he's against us," Evie mused. "I think he just places his homeworld as a higher priority than ours."

"That makes sense," I admitted. "I would do the same in his position. Hell, I was in this position, and I did the same thing. But Rouhr and I had an agreement. I don't like that Thribb is trying to force Rouhr to break that agreement behind my back."

"Rouhr came down hard on the strike team members," Evie explained. "I don't think Thribb was officially punished, though. Sakev said he'd never heard Rouhr lose his temper the way he did. Sakev didn't see anything, but it sounded like Rouhr physically fought someone."

"Holy crap," I gasped. "Where's Rouhr now?"

I already knew the answer before Evie said it.

"He went into his office, and he hasn't come out yet. Not even to eat."

Exactly as I suspected.

"I'm going to get him on the comm and invite him

back here," I decided. "I think it'll reinforce the idea that the people here still need help."

"Don't lie," Evie said in a knowing voice. "You want him there to make sure he eats, sleeps, and doesn't drive himself crazy. You're hiding behind work and you know it."

I did know it.

But I sure as hell wasn't going to admit it.

"Bye, Evie," I sang into the comm link before hanging up.

I fiddled with the comm settings, looking for the private channel he'd used to call me before the cure strike started.

Years ago, it felt like. Decades.

There.

Maybe.

"Rouhr, come in?" I crossed my fingers.

"Is that you, Vidia?" His voice crackled through. "Is everything alright?"

"Yes," I hesitated for a moment, wondering if the conversation was private or not, how much I should say. "I heard things got tense earlier today."

"A bit," he admitted. "The situation is taking a toll on everyone."

"Yes, it is," I agreed. "I have a proposition."

"I've been doing a bit of research on human

metaphors," he teased. *We better be on a private channel*, I fumed, cheeks heating.

"Come back to Glymna for the night," I pushed on. "Get away from Thribb, the strike teams, and that stupid cot in your office. I promise it'll do you some good before the next cure strike."

I had another three arguments prepared in case he refused, but to my surprise, he didn't.

"Very well," he agreed.

"What?" My surprise was obvious enough to make Rouhr laugh.

"Getting away from everyone for a little while is exactly what I need," he repeated. "I'll clean up and ask Fen to open a rift."

"Great!" I exclaimed. "I'll see you soon."

"See you soon."

It was a makeshift hospital in the middle of an imperiled city during an invasion.

But it was still a date.

ROUHR

For the first time in my entire military career, I was glad to be away from my crew.

Standing in the city square with Vidia, looking at all the people we were helping, only reinforced my belief that I'd made the right choice.

I was disappointed with my men for not seeing how important our work here was.

Somewhere, I must have failed them.

But I wasn't going to think about that any more today.

"I didn't think you were going to come," Vidia confessed.

"Really?" I was surprised. "Why?"

"You're a lot like me," she explained. "We don't like

to leave our work unless we are forcibly dragged away. Your work is on the *Aurora*."

"It's here now, too," I said. "Whether you like it or not, I'm invested in what happens to these people."

"I like it very much." Vidia smiled up at me, the soft happiness on her face soothing all of the irritations of the day away.

She was magic.

I laced my fingers through hers, marveling at how tiny her hands were. "I also came to see you, you know?" I said softly.

A deep blush bloomed over her cheeks, and she leaned close to rest her head on my arm.

"I know we both have mountains of work to do," she said. "But I want," she stopped, started again, "I'd like to make time for you, for us, for a change."

Oh. My brave little human.

"I'd like nothing better." I wondered what we would've been like if we'd met when we were younger, less weighed down by the burden of our responsibilities.

But Vidia was an intelligent woman. And I could see in her eyes as she looked at me that she understood my position as well.

We were in the middle of a war. There were events that were transpiring larger than us. But through it all, whatever time we would have left, we would do our best to make it for each other.

Compared to that understanding, our words seemed small.

Suddenly, a young woman rushed up to Vidia looking flustered and worried.

"Vidia, we need your help," she pleaded. "People keep getting sent to the wrong places. Names are getting mixed up. It's a disaster."

"I'll be right there," Vidia soothed the girl.

She turned to me and winked.

"Well, that was fast. I won't be long." She let the frantic girl pull her back to the tables at the center of the city square.

I stood alone, looking around at all the people. A tall, reed-thin man caught my eye. His skin was so pale, I knew he had to be one of the survivors.

He struggled to rise from a bench, as if his limbs wouldn't listen to his commands. I rushed to help him, grateful that I'd remembered to wear my holo-disguise.

"Are you all right?" I asked, extending a hand toward him but not yet touching him.

"Leg hurts," the man groaned.

I let him make the decision to grab my arm. He gripped my forearm and my shoulder and then hauled himself up. He held tight until he could stand steady.

"Let me help you to one of the doctors," I suggested. "Have you been seen at all yet?"

"Saw doctor hours ago," he explained in halting speech. His voice was scratchy with disuse. "Leg is only bruised. Will heal by itself."

"I see," I nodded. "Have you been assigned a cot? I could help you get back to it."

"Have a cot," he grunted. "Sitting here to wait."

"Waiting for what?" I asked.

"Wife," he answered, glancing around hopefully.

"Do you remember the last time you saw her?" I asked, fearing the worst.

"Not since before those bug things attacked." He cleared his throat. "We escaped our town with others, but they caught us anyway."

Many of the humans in similar situations to this man ended up as hybrids. It was possible that his wife was here somewhere or in one of the other camps.

Far better than any of the alternatives.

"There were a considerable amount of people suffering from memory loss," I explained. "Your wife could be one of them. If not, my team and I are performing two more rescues in the coming days. Your wife could be in one of the other camps."

"Do you think so?" he asked, turning to look me in the eyes.

"Giant bugs fell through the sky and are attacking

the planet," I forced a laugh. "After that, I don't think anything is beyond the realm of possibility."

The man smiled. "That's a good way to look at it," he nodded. "I'll look and see where the helpers put the people with memory loss."

"That's a good place to start," I replied. "Let me know when you find her, will you?"

The man nodded and waved before hobbling toward the central tables.

Vidia would point him in the right direction, figure out what he needed.

She always did.

"That right there is why the dark-haired girl likes you," a voice startled me.

A tiny old woman, her head barely level with my chest, appeared at my side.

I hadn't heard her approach.

It was getting easier to sneak up on me, apparently.

"What?" I asked.

The woman's skin wasn't pale. She wasn't too thin. I didn't think she had been a hybrid.

"The way you talk to people, the way you help them," the woman clarified, "that's why she likes you."

I laughed uneasily. I had no idea what to say.

"What are you planning on doing about it?" she asked, prodding my chest with her bony finger.

"What?" I couldn't help but laugh, but forced myself

to stop as soon as I saw the hard look of determination on her wrinkled face.

"You've got to do something about it," she insisted. "Listen to me, young man. My late husband and I met right here in the city square. We met here every day for a month before he finally did something. If he had waited even one more day, I would've walked away."

"Lucky for him he figured it out," I smiled.

"Damn right!" she exclaimed. "Do you know what he did?"

"No, but I'm sure you'll enlighten me." I was fully prepared to humor this old woman.

And who knew? She might be able to point me in the right direction with Vidia.

"He took me to the crystal caverns," she declared proudly. "It was the second-best night of my life."

"Only the second?" I laughed.

"The wedding night blew it out of the water," she cackled.

I laughed along heartily.

"Rouhr, I'm glad to see you're making friends," Vidia's voice floated into my ears.

When I looked at her, she was smiling from ear to ear. "How are you today, Demi?"

"I'm just fine, my dear," the old woman replied. "And I wouldn't say I'm acting as a friend."

"Oh?" Vidia's eyebrows shot up. "What would you say you're acting as?"

"A guide. A mentor, if you will," Demi said with a flourish.

"Wow." Vidia placed her hands on her hips. "Care to elaborate?"

"He has something to ask you." Demi jerked her head in my direction.

Vidia looked to me expectantly.

"Vidia," I said in an overly formal tone, deeply aware of our audience, "would you like to go to the crystal caverns with me?"

"Yes." She didn't even hesitate.

"You're welcome!" Demi called before hobbling away.

"What an unusual woman."

I watched her disappear into the crowd.

"Demi is the best," Vidia beamed. "Do you really want to go to the caverns?"

"Of course," I assured her. "I just don't know where they are. Or if you have time."

"Lucky for you, I do." Vidia took me by the hand and led me through the winding paths of the city inside the mountain.

The caverns were all the way in the back of the city, the entrance just a set of winding stairs that went down into pitch blackness. I went down first, constantly reaching back to help Vidia down as the light faded away.

We climbed down in the darkness for a few moments before a dull blue light appeared from below.

"What is that?" I asked.

"You'll see!" I could sense her excitement even if I couldn't see her face.

The dull light grew brighter and brighter until it lit up everything around us. Once we were on level ground, I could see where the light came from. The caverns were massive and covered in bioluminescent crystal formations.

Vidia glowed in the ethereal lights, brilliant, fragile, strong-willed.

Mine.

Before I could think twice, I took her hands in mine and pulled her closer to me, my fingers winding through her hair, pulling her body tight against me.

With a surprised squeak, she opened her mouth to mine, letting me taste her, drink her in.

I'd never have enough.

Especially since--

I broke away, silently cursing myself.

"My apologies," I looked away, anywhere but in the depths of her fascinating eyes. "I don't know what came over me. I'd arrest a soldier for behaving in such a--"

She leaned forward, her lips teasing at mine as she wrapped her arms around my neck.

"You should hush now," she murmured as she nuzzled the scales of my neck. My mutinous hands tightened against her back.

"Did you really just tell a general to hush," I asked between kisses. This was madness, but I couldn't care, not when she was here, with me, no cares or worries to interrupt us.

"We have so few moments to be alone, so little time before..." she explained. "I don't want to waste a single second of it pretending I care less than I do."

The truth of her words sliced me like a knife, but I wouldn't dishonor it, dishonor her, by pretending not to understand.

I kissed her harder, pressing myself against her.

She let out a soft gasp when she realized how aroused I was becoming.

I couldn't remember the last time I'd felt such intensity.

True desire.

"I feel the same," I sighed against her mouth.

I wound one hand into her soft, thick hair again and brought her mouth to mine, leaving the other to caress her side, knead the lush curves of her hip. Our tongues danced together as we kissed, her sweet taste indescribable.

Addicting.

Her breasts pressed against my chest, her body folded against mine. "Rouhr," she moaned against my lips, inflaming the deep primal instinct inside me.

I needed her. I had to have her *now*.

A rattling noise echoed down the staircase, followed by voices. More people were entering the caverns.

Of course they were. We were in a public place, and I was moments from ravaging her.

I'd promised to protect the civilians of this world, but right now, I'd be tempted to reconsider.

My breath still ragged, my blood pounded through my veins as I struggled to compose myself.

Vidia looked like she was having difficulties, as well. Her hair was tousled, and her lips were lush and swollen from kissing.

It would be obvious to anyone what we'd been doing.

She led me deeper into the caverns for a few moments while we cooled down, letting the shadows cover the signs of our adventure.

The massive crystals were a sight to behold, but not nearly as beautiful as Vidia.

After half an hour or so, we climbed back up the stairs and walked back to the main part of the city.

"It's a damn shame those people showed up," Vidia sighed as we reemerged into the bustle.

"We'll have our time together." I squeezed her hand. "I promise."

VIDIA

It simply wasn't meant to be our night.

I could organize a city, plan a rescue mission, convince politicians to do damn near anything...but have a quiet date?

Apparently not.

After we left the crystal caverns, I invited Rouhr to share the room I'd rented for the night. It wasn't the same inn as before.

This one, The Mountain Inn, was much smaller and more crowded.

I brought Rouhr up to the room with every intention of continuing what we'd started down in the caverns, but every kiss and gentle sigh shared between us was punctuated by a shout from someone else or a loud bang from the kitchen.

The walls were thin.

Very thin.

We could hear the sounds of people drinking and dining in the tavern below and the guests in the rooms on either side of us.

I let out a frustrated sigh and rested my forehead against Rouhr's bare chest.

He'd deactivated his holo-disguise as soon as we'd closed the door to the room.

"This isn't what I had in mind," I laughed.

"Me, either," Rouhr admitted.

Someone bumped into the wall of our room hard enough to rattle the dresser pushed up against it.

That prompted another round of laughter between Rouhr and me.

"Let's just try to sleep, then?" I suggested but wasn't even sure that would work. I'd booked the room for a single person, so I'd been given a bed for a single person.

A single human.

"I can always go back to the ship and sleep there," Rouhr offered.

"This is supposed to be your night away from the *Aurora*," I insisted. "We'll make this work."

After some careful maneuvering, we found a comfortable position.

Rouhr lay on his back, taking up most of the mattress. I was wedged against his side, tucked under his arm. His chest was my pillow.

"You're right. This is perfect," he sighed, squeezing me closer to him.

We both slept soundly that night.

Waking up the next morning was one of the happiest moments of my life.

When I remembered I was curled against Rouhr's side and not a pillow, my body filled with a giddy warmth. It wasn't the electric zap that often accompanied the excitement of a new relationship.

Instead, it was a natural sense of belonging. I was exactly where I was supposed to be with the person I was supposed to be with.

Certain and sure.

I was too old for that breathless, almost chaotic rush of a thousand feelings that came with the sense of infinite possibility.

I felt young for being in the middle of my forties, happy to be smart enough to know that the chaotic rush didn't always lead to happily ever after.

But this moment in time, I had to grasp with both hands.

Whatever else the day held for us, and whatever else the next several days, weeks, and months would grant us, I needed to acknowledge that I was happy waking up next to Rouhr.

I nudged Rouhr awake. I felt guilty for it. He never slept this much. I hated to disturb him, but there was simply too much we needed to get done today.

"Hmm," he groaned.

His arms tightened around me.

"Time to get up." I planted small kisses where my face was pressed against his chest.

"Skrell." His body went slack.

"That's the first time I've ever heard you curse," I laughed. "You must really not want to get up."

"I really don't," he admitted. "This is why I never sleep for very long. I don't want to realize how much I love sleeping."

"Your logic is flawed." I wiggled out of his arms and stood up beside the bed. "Come on." I grabbed his arm and tugged. It was like trying to move the mountain itself. "We have lives to save!"

"I'm getting up, I'm getting up!" he exclaimed.

He let himself slide over the sheets, reaching for one last kiss before I danced away.

We took turns washing up in the tiny bathing room. There was no way for two people to stand inside at once. Poor Rouhr had a difficult time maneuvering when it was just himself.

We rushed out of the inn before the innkeeper could

ask if we'd enjoyed our stay. I wasn't sure that even as a politician I'd be able to give an answer that wouldn't leave me blushing all day.

The city square was nearly empty compared to yesterday. There was still a line of survivors waiting to see the doctors. Some were walking around the square, the gentle exercise a first step towards bringing their bodies back to normal.

"I met a man here yesterday before Demi and I started talking," Rouhr commented. "He was looking for his wife, but I don't see him here. I hope he found her."

"I'm sure he did," I said brightly. Things were finally going right for these people since the Xathi fell through the rift.

I liked to think that anything was possible.

The *Aurora* was bustling with activity when we arrived in preparation for the next cure strike.

"I'm going to make sure Evie and Leena have everything they need." I gave Rouhr's hand a quick squeeze before making my way toward the labs.

I struggled to switch from my giddy-and-falling-in-love mindset into my work mindset.

"I can't believe Rouhr won't let us go," a voice grumbled off to my right.

He sounded angry.

"Not using every man he's got for these cure strikes

is just foolish."

"All because we asked to go home sooner," another voice said bitterly.

This must've had something to do with what Evie told me yesterday. She mentioned that Rouhr had come down hard on a few of the crew members.

I slowed my pace to listen more.

"At least we'll be going home," the first one sighed.

I wanted to look to see who it was, but I didn't want to draw attention to the fact that I was eavesdropping on a private conversation.

"Don't get your hopes up too high," the second cautioned. "The *Aurora* might not be stable enough to handle space travel. Rouhr's warned us about it a hundred times."

"I've been talking to Thribb," the first said. "He says the *Aurora* will definitely fly again. But if she can't handle space travel, we can potentially still be operational in our journey simply because we have the Gateway. We won't need to be in space for long at all."

"You think we're going to take the Gateway with us?" the second asked.

"Of course! What would the humans need it for?" the first scoffed.

"Good point."

I hadn't given much thought to what would happen to the Gateway when this was all over.

I guess I hadn't given much thought to anything. I hurried away from the conversation.

I'd heard enough.

An ache formed in my chest.

I knew Rouhr would leave one day. One day soon, if all went according to plan.

Rouhr had promised that he wouldn't leave while the planet still needed his help. I knew he would keep his word. The fact that he'd punished those crew members proved that he was committed to saving this planet.

I wasn't stupid enough to believe that Rouhr would make Ankau his permanent home.

We'd been friends for a while now. Only recently had something more than friendship developed between us.

It wasn't enough to give up a decorated military career, a dedicated crew, and a war that was still raging on the other side of the universe.

It couldn't be.

Being wrapped up in his arms, sharing our first kisses, and feeling that complete sense of belonging had muddled the reality of our situation.

Rouhr was going to leave, and it was going to hurt. A lot.

Even if I'd decided to ignore reality for the time we had together, I needed to start preparing myself for it now. If I kept myself in denial for the remainder of Rouhr's time here, it would only make things worse.

Even when the planet was safe from the Xathi, I would still have work to do.

But I couldn't shake the feeling that even with our time limited, I needed to consciously grasp every moment I had with Rouhr.

Waking up next to him this morning was heaven.

And if we really had as little time as I thought, I would avail myself of those moments as much as I could, but without losing myself again.

The people that were relocated to Glymna would need permanent homes.

Doctors from all over would need to be taught how to spot the signs of hybridism, just in case someone had a relapse.

The cities and towns needed to be rebuilt.

Healing the damage done by the Xathi would be a long process, one that deserved my full attention.

I couldn't risk letting heartbreak distract me from it.

I took a deep, shuddering breath and buried the pain and sadness deep down for me to deal with another time. I would continue to be Rouhr's friend. He deserved that much.

I would do everything to enjoy this moment with Rouhr—regardless of how limited our time was or was not.

I had made up my mind.

Now the hard part was going to be in carrying it out and not retreating into myself.

ROUHR

As the strikes teams and I moved through the thick clouds of pink mist, I looked up at the sky. This time, no air unit lingered behind the others.

Good.

Perhaps Vidia finally realized that putting herself in harm's way wasn't the best way to get things done.

It made me worried, knowing she was within potential range for an attack.

But a small part of me was disappointed that she wasn't up in the sky, fighting with D'val to let her stay behind and help.

The Xathi queen obviously expected another attack on her camps. There were nearly thirty Xathi guarding this one, enough that I had to wonder how many soldiers she had left on the planet.

Were the hybrids such an important part of her strategy?

This camp was a few miles south of Duvest, a city the Xathi queen had shown interest in before.

Her minions had dealt a considerable amount of damage to the city in the initial attack, but it hadn't fallen. Duvest was actually where we had first put the neuro-grenades into action, with positive results.

There'd been debate over using those same neuro-grenades, as well as our newly developed scent-grenades, in our cure strikes.

But after we saw the effect the sonic barrier had on the hybrids, it was decided we wouldn't use any weapons that had the potential to harm the recovering humans affected by the cure.

Our attack on the Xathi guards was almost identical to our attack on the guards at the last camp. The snipers hung back and disabled the Xathi from afar. The heavy hitters rushed in, using the low visibility to their advantage.

I took great pleasure in waiting for the perfect moment to blow holes clean through the Xathi's crystal exteriors. This time, no Xathi got the chance to knock me to the ground.

We supplemented the strike team members currently on probation with promising members of the ground teams.

If Karzin, Rokul, and the others kept up their insubordinate behavior, I knew exactly with whom I'd replace them.

We made quick work of the Xathi. The pink mist of the cure was different than it was last time. It had dissipated relatively quickly during the first strike. Now, it hung in thick, cloud-like clusters.

Apparently, our scientific team had made good use of our notes for them.

It totally blinded the Xathi. None of them could pinpoint exactly where we were as we attacked from outside the cloud.

"That wasn't as satisfying as I thought it would be," Dax huffed as he yanked out an arrow that was deeply embedded in the head of a dead Xathi.

"I know what you mean," Sakev replied. "We're getting too used to fighting them."

"You say that like it's a bad thing," I chuckled. "Would you like me to drop you off at the entrance to the Xathi ship? Would that be more exciting?"

"Would you, General?" Axtin rested his hammer across his shoulders. "I still have some unfinished business there."

Some time ago, Axtin had led the charge into the belly of the Xathi ship to rescue Leena and other humans that the Xathi held captive. One of which was a little girl who'd become part of his and Leena's family.

She was fine now, but I'd heard she still had nightmares.

"We all do," Vrehx added.

"We'll get our chance," Tu'ver assured them.

"We'd better," Sk'lar's tone was grim.

"We'll take them down after we finish crippling their forces," I said. "Taking away their hybrids is a good start to that. Now, let's get these poor people to Glymna."

There were more in this camp than there had been in the first. I assumed Vidia was already in Glymna, waiting. I switched to her comm channel.

"Sending survivors through shortly," I explained. "Let the doctors and volunteers know they should be prepared for more people than last time."

"Understood," she said briskly before clicking off the channel.

That was strange.

Usually, Vidia had hundreds of questions.

Evie and Leena had made modifications to this batch of the cure. Didn't Vidia want to know how it went?

I put it out of my mind. She was probably in the middle of something else and didn't have time to talk. I'd certainly done the same any number of times.

She'd track me down as soon as I entered Glymna.

My crew made quick work of the hybrids that

weren't affected by the cure. There'd been around thirty at the last camp. At this camp, there were only twenty.

The cure appeared to work faster this time, more effectively, as well.

The crystal coating on people's skin was easier to chip away. The humans seemed to come to their senses a little bit faster, although more people had blotchy red skin where the cure had touched them directly.

An allergic reaction, I'd been told. And one I was sure the victims would be willing to risk.

Once I was sure all threats had been eliminated, I pulled out my comm again.

"Fen, open the rift to Glymna, please," I ordered.

"Yes, General," a voice replied.

It wasn't Fen.

"Amira, is that you?"

"It is!" She sounded so excited. "Fen wanted a break from being everyone's personal doorman into space. She's letting me control the Gateway."

A shimmering rift opened, with the city square of Glymna on the other side.

"Excellent."

I smiled, although I knew she couldn't see it.

Several of the survivors recognized Glymna and didn't hesitate in going through the rift, but many were still apprehensive. Of course, the only rift they'd seen before was the one that their tormentors had fallen through.

A few of my crew went through to assist the survivors that had already crossed into Glymna. The rest of us stayed behind to coax the hesitant ones.

One survivor, a young woman that looked similar in age to Vidia's friend Hannah, was too exhausted to move. She lay down on the ground and desperately tried to sleep, but every time she closed her eyes, she became afraid.

"Let me help," I said softly. "Right on the other side of that rift is a doctor who will give you medicine. There are citizens who will feed you and a nice bed where you can sleep for days if you want to."

It took some patience. Eventually, I got her to put her arms around my neck so I could carry her through the rift.

I took her right to the designated area for survivors that were worse off than the others. I sat with her, talking to her and telling her stories about whatever random thing I could think of. I needed to distract her until I placed her in the arms of one of the doctors.

As she was carried away, I realized I hadn't gotten her name. I wondered if she knew it herself. I swore I'd keep an eye out for her when she came out of the examination room.

Until then, I wanted to find Vidia. Even if she was

too busy to talk, I was sure she could use an extra pair of hands to boss around.

I found her in the center of the square where the volunteer tables were set up. She was scrolling through two datapads at the same time, her jaw set with determination.

"Vidia." I smiled when I approached her.

I knew something wasn't right when she didn't smile back.

"What's wrong?" I asked.

"Nothing," she said quickly. "Aside from the hundreds of people in need of medical attention," she added.

A tinge of humor touched her voice, but it didn't sound right. Strained, forced.

"Let me know how I can help," I said.

"Preparing for the next strike would be the most productive thing you could do," she replied without looking up from her datapads.

Something was definitely wrong. Just yesterday, she was putting me to work and urging me to stay as long as I could. Now it felt like she didn't want me here.

"Are you sure everything is alright?" I asked again.

She let out a short sigh and picked up the two datapads, as well as a handful of others.

"Everything is all right, I'm just very busy." She

flashed a quick, fake smile, before walking away from the table.

I followed her. I didn't believe for a second that everything was all right.

"Whatever it is, you can tell me," I said to her back since she wouldn't walk beside me. "I'm sure I can help."

"I appreciate the offer," she replied.

That, at least, sounded like normal Vidia.

"But there's nothing I need help with. I'd actually prefer to be alone."

I reached out and gently grabbed Vidia's arm, forcing her to stop and look at me.

Skrell. Tears welled in her eyes.

"If you tell me what it is, I promise I'll let you be alone," I said. "But I need you to tell me, so I won't worry all day."

"I told you, nothing's wrong!" She tried to jerk her arm out of my grip.

"I don't know how you expect me to believe that when you're acting like this," I said.

A terrible thought crossed my mind. "Was there an attack here? Did the Xathi queen have more control over the survivors than we thought?"

I whirled around, pushing Vidia behind me, all senses stretched and alert, ready for an attack.

Why hadn't I heard about it?

I shouldn't have been in the field, cut off from the reports.

Cut off from protecting her.

"You're being ridiculous," Vidia snapped.

I surveyed the square again. Everyone seemed busy, but calm. The air wasn't filled with the scent of fear.

No one was acting under duress.

The Xathi weren't here.

But then... An attack from an enemy I understood was preferable to this mysterious tension rolling off her.

I narrowed my eyes, checked her once again for an injury. How could humans be so delicate? Why didn't I insist she stay on the *Aurora*?

She pushed me away gently. "I'm just in a bad mood," she sighed. "Isn't that allowed?"

"Of course, it is," I said suspiciously. Vidia didn't do bad moods, not in all the time I'd known her.

Tired, frustrated? Sure.

But a general bad mood?

Never.

"I think there's more to it than that."

"Well, there's not."

But as she spoke, a tear slipped down her cheek. I reached to wipe it away, and she finally relaxed, shoulders slumping as she stood before me.

"Tell me," I whispered.

She tipped her face upward to stop the tears from falling, eyes not meeting mine.

There was a moment of silence on her part. Then, she looked at me.

"It's just so hard being near you when I know you're going to leave in the end," she sighed. "I thought I could handle it, but I can't. I'm sorry."

Her words shocked me, as hard as any enemy's blow.

She slipped away from me and disappeared into the crowded square.

Leaving me alone.

Once again, just me and my duty.

VIDIA

My eyes stung, as if full of sand, and my chest felt shredded between ragged gasps.

Why did Rouhr have to fight me so hard when I asked to be left alone?

Of course, I knew the answer to that already.

Because he cared.

Had our roles been reversed, I would've done the same thing.

Rouhr was never supposed to know how upset I was.

I thought I'd be able to pretend better, to smile, be his friend again.

Not have every moment he was near a bitter reminder of how little time we had left.

I realized how silly it was for me to hope that Rouhr

would simply allow our relationship to revert to friendship.

Anything more would break my heart.

I was stupid for hoping it would be that easy.

Cowardly. Foolish.

And now the damage was done. Rouhr knew how I felt about him leaving. He'd be smart enough not to entangle himself.

I knew the score. I shouldn't have let myself fall so hard.

He didn't need that sort of distraction, not when he was fighting to save my planet and then lead his men back to a war in their home galaxy.

Away from Ankau.

Away from me.

I walked around the square in a daze. There were a million things I needed to get done in time for tomorrow's third and final cure strike.

And I couldn't focus on any of them.

Thankfully, the doctors had found their own rhythm for examining patients. They knew exactly what to look for now. A handful of hybridism relapses were caught and handled immediately upon discovery with stronger doses.

The volunteers were quickly becoming professionals in dealing with nervous and distressed survivors.

I was amazed by the number of residents who had generously opened their homes to the survivors. Some people were only able to take one or two survivors. Others, who lived in huge houses, were able to take as many as ten.

I didn't realize how many hours had passed when one of the volunteers found me and told me I was receiving a call on one of the comm units. I rushed to answer. I hadn't been wearing a comm link all day.

If someone on the *Aurora* needed me, they wouldn't have been able to reach me.

"Hello?" I put the comm unit to my ear.

"Vidia, where are you?" It was Evie.

"I'm in Glymna," I replied. "Why, is everything okay?"

"Yeah, everything is fine in the lab," she said quickly. "But Rouhr's been in a low mood. I haven't seen you in a while, thought you might know what was going on."

I winced.

"Oh." I scrambled for something to say. "I'm going to be staying here another night. There's a lot that needs to be done before the people from the third hybrid camp arrive here."

"I bet," Evie agreed. There was a pause before she spoke again. "Are you alright? You seem a little off."

"I'm just tired, that's all." I forced some perkiness

into my voice to convince her. "I've been running around like a crazy person all day."

"Okay," Evie said slowly. "Well, make sure to take time to focus on your needs. Remember to eat, get plenty of sleep."

"Yes, Mom." I rolled my eyes, even though Evie couldn't see me.

I turned off the comm unit and handed it back to the volunteer. I was grateful to have a friend like Evie.

But that didn't mean I was going to listen to her advice.

I worked late into the night and slept for a few fitful hours in the same inn Rouhr and I had slept in the previous night.

The memories of what might have been kept me tossing and turning.

In the morning, I was groggy and irritated. The last thing I wanted was to go back to the *Aurora*.

But I didn't want to miss out on the final cure strike. This was what we'd been working toward for so long.

I borrowed a comm to contact Fen, so she could open a rift for me. When I stepped onto the main deck of the *Aurora*, the first thing I did was look for Rouhr. I couldn't bear seeing him yet.

"There you are!" I heard Evie's voice coming up behind me.

I smiled weakly, unable to match her brightness.

"You look like crap. I told you not to overwork yourself."

"You know me," I shrugged, thankful that my bad habits were enough to cover up my real distress. "I can't help it."

"Clearly." Evie shoved her thermos full of coffee into my hand. "Drink. You need it more than I do. Before we take off, I want to show you something. I think it'll make you happy."

Evie gently dragged me as I drank her coffee, finally pulling me into a small office adjacent to Rouhr's.

My heart sped up, but thankfully, he wasn't inside.

"Look!" She gestured proudly to a map of our planet.

Half of the small cities were circled in pale blue. There were other markings in various colors. I didn't know what any of them meant.

"What am I looking at exactly?" I asked.

Evie let out an exasperated sigh.

"The areas circled in blue are certified Xathi-free!" she declared. "Everyone inside has been given the pills, and the Urai have set up sonic barriers."

"That's amazing!" My eyes went wide as I realized how much work Evie and the Urai crew had done between cure strikes. "We're taking back our planet."

"Yes, we are," Evie grinned. "Remember those hybrid patrols we wanted to attract to the main camps?"

"Yes." I'd been so focused on helping people from the camps, I'd entirely forgotten about the rest of the plan.

Focused on the people, and on Rouhr, to be honest.

But that was over now.

"Some of those patrols were closing in on these towns. Yesterday, Sakev got bored and started chucking cure canisters at them. I yelled at him for it at first, but it actually worked. He's off the hook for being impulsive," she laughed. "For now."

"Where are the people from the patrols now?" I asked. "They haven't been sent to Glymna."

"They're recovering within the safe zones." Evie tapped on one of the blue-circled cities. "I taught people in each town how to treat hybridism. I gave them the number to the comm unit in my office, so they can call me in case anything goes wrong."

"It's amazing how much you were able to accomplish." I was in awe.

"Traveling by Gateway saves so much time," Evie said. "Imagine how much we could've accomplished by now if we'd had it from the beginning."

"We'd have rebuilt our planet ten times over," I chuckled, "if we'd had the Gateway, and the sonic barrier. And the cure. It's a long list, but finally we have an edge."

Evie and I stared at the board for a few moments,

looking at all that had been accomplished and all that still needed to be done.

"We better get down to the docking bay before they leave without us." Evie broke the silence.

"Right." Anxiety bubbled in my stomach.

Or maybe it was just the coffee.

Evie drank really strong coffee.

Everyone was gathered in the docking bay. When I arrived, I grabbed my cure canisters, my comm, and my vision goggles, then slid into my seat in D'val's transport unit before he was in his pilot's seat.

"You're in a hurry today," he commented when he climbed into his seat in front of me.

"Aren't you?" I replied. "This is the last one. Then we're done."

"Not quite," D'val corrected. "We still have to deal with the Xathi."

"I don't think I'll be allowed to join in that fight," I chuckled weakly.

D'val laughed as well.

"Yeah, the general probably isn't going to bend on that one. Either way, it was nice working with you."

"Nice working with you, too." I gave him a friendly pat on the shoulder.

We lifted off and flew through the Gateway, so that we were positioned above the third camp. This camp was only three miles from where the *Vengeance* had crashed. No one knew why the Xathi had picked this spot for a camp.

"Drop your canisters," Evie ordered.

I had two this time. I pulled the tabs and dropped them one after the other through the chute over the side of the unit.

"Let's go," I said to D'val.

"Don't you want to watch anything?"

"Not today," I replied. "I have too much to do."

"If you say so." He flew us back to the *Aurora*.

This time we were the first ones back.

"See you around," I said to him before turning in my vision goggles.

I kept the comm on me, so I would know when to expect more survivors in Glymna. I asked Fen to open a rift and swiftly left the *Aurora*.

I threw myself into my work. I fetched blankets for cots, helped a few confused survivors from the last rescue find family members and places to stay, relocated those who were ready to move out of the hospital wards--any chore that needed to be done.

When a rift opened in the middle of the city square, I was prepared. Newly cured people flooded through, looking dazed and confused. I directed them to the doctors, who were ready and waiting. So far, none of the crew had come through with them.

"Don't worry," I soothed a frantic elderly man. "Just

let the doctors help you. Then we can figure out where your son is. He's probably already being examined."

The blaring tone of my comm startled everyone around me.

"Sorry," I said to everyone as I clicked the comm to the right frequency. "Yes?"

"Vidia, where are you?" Evie sounded panicked.

"What's wrong?" Every inch of me was immediately on edge.

"The Xathi ambushed the strike teams at the third camp," she said breathlessly.

"What?" I looked toward the rift.

People were still streaming through. The strike teams must have handled the Xathi, or else they wouldn't have asked Fen to open a rift.

So why the urgency in her voice?

"They defeated them," Evie explained. "But some of the crew are missing."

"Missing?" That could only be bad.

A Xathi ambush and now missing crew members.

"Is it Sakev?"

"No, Sakev is with me now," Evie sounded relieved for a moment before her voice turned pinched and tight again.

"Vidia, Rouhr is missing."

ROUHR

The third cure strike didn't go according to plan.

The Xathi were clearly anticipating us.

Once the cure dropped, the Xathi didn't chase after us through the mist.

They went after the humans, killing them even as the crystal shards fell to the ground.

The strike teams charged, ripping the Xathi Soldiers and Hunters away from their prey.

But in the chaos, they didn't notice a large group of newly-cured humans climbing out of the pen and running into the forest.

I grabbed the two team members closest to me, both from the ground teams filling in for the strike team members who were serving their punishments.

I signaled to them to follow me, and we ran after the panicked humans.

A Xathi tried to stop us, sideswiping me hard enough to send me reeling. But it was no match for the three of us. In minutes we'd finished it, but the band of humans had disappeared into the forest.

We caught up to one fairly quickly, a young woman who'd badly twisted her ankle while running panicked.

One of the ground team members, Xad, picked her up and carried her as we searched for the others. We had to find them before the Xathi or any of the local wildlife did.

Neither would be forgiving, and in their weakened states, even if the humans were as experienced as Jeneva, they wouldn't survive long.

After a few minutes of searching, I lifted my comm to check in with the rest of the team. We could use their assistance, once the majority of the survivors had been sent through the rift.

But only a piece came up in my hand.

"Skrell," I muttered. The Xathi must've cracked it when it sideswiped me. "Either of you have your comm?"

Both of them shook their heads.

What the-

Right.

Although a comm was part of standard operating uniforms, we'd lost so much equipment during the evacuation of the *Vengeance,* they were limited now.

And apparently the replacement team members hadn't been issued a set.

An oversight on my part.

I cursed myself. How many other things had I overlooked during my infatuation with Vidia?

Maybe it was for the best she'd pulled away from me.

And maybe the empty feeling in my gut would fade in time.

Sure it would.

"What should we do, General?" Xad asked.

"Let's keep searching for the humans," I ordered. "They can't have gone far. Once we find as many as we can, we'll take them to a safe space."

"But how?" the other ground team member, Bane, asked. "We can't comm for a rift."

"Should we go back to the pen?" Xad asked. "The rest of the teams would look for us there, and we can regroup, search in larger numbers."

"No," I replied. "The humans can't be left alone out here. I've known the Xathi to spread out from the main force, so there may be marauding Hunters."

There was silence.

"We'll figure it out," I assured them. "First step, find the humans."

Despite spending weeks, or even months, in a hybrid state, the newly-cured humans hadn't lost their natural pack mentality. We found clusters of them huddled together within a few square miles of the hybrid camp.

Eventually, we herded them into one group. Any reserves of energy they'd had were expended escaping the attacking Xathi, and now they lay exhausted on the forest floor.

"They won't get much farther without food and water," I said to Xad and Bane.

Thanks to Jeneva's field guide, I recognized a few of the fruit and flower-bearing plants. "You two concentrate on making the water drinkable. I'll handle the food."

Ironically, the only safe berry looked as if it was rotting from the inside out. The skin was a dull black color, and if the skin was punctured, it would ooze green mush. But she swore it tasted like honey, and contained a surprising amount of nutrients.

"They look disgusting, but they aren't," I assured the skeptical humans. To prove it, I popped one in my mouth and smiled. I waited until a few of them had tried it for themselves before going back into the forest to find more food. From the reports of the cured, hybrids weren't allowed to sleep, so I doubted they were allowed to eat much, either. A handful of berries wasn't going to be enough for them.

High up in the trees, I spied a variety of fruit. I couldn't remember all the varieties off the top of my head, but I knew the oblong fruits with bright blue and pink stripes were safe to ingest. As part of my uniform, I kept a large knife as a weapon on my person whenever I was in the field. I also had a much smaller blade meant to be used as a tool in survival situations.

I buried the blade of the large knife deep into the wood of the tree and pulled myself up. There were many branches to grab on to when needed, as well as small knots in the bark that made decent footholds. I didn't trust the smaller knife to bear my full weight, so I held it between my teeth until I needed it.

Up in the canopy, there were dozens of pink and blue fruits, each one half the length of my arm. I hoped they were ripe, but I didn't think it would make a difference to the humans below. I took the small knife out of my mouth, and used it to cut the fruits free from their vines, letting them fall to the forest floor below. I sliced until there was no more of that fruit in my immediate area.

I climbed back down to begin gathering them. Most

of them had survived the fall with little damage. A few were cracked open. The insides of the fruits were pure white. Curious, I picked up a broken piece and took a bite. It was bitter. It seemed these weren't quite ripe yet.

I carried five at a time back to the camp, and placed them next to the nearly depleted berry piles. I used the large knife to cut them open so the humans could scoop out the soft insides. One of the humans eagerly reached for the new fruit, but his expression changed to one of disgust as soon as he tasted it. At first, I was worried they would refuse the food, but the human had an idea.

He picked up a few of the black berries and squished them in his hand to make a pulp. He then spread it across the white flesh of the fruit. When he took another bite, he smiled and gestured to the others.

"Good thinking," I commended him. "Can you speak? Can anyone speak?"

"Hurts," he croaked and rubbed his throat where I could still see the remnants of the crystalline prison.

"Of course," I nodded. "Forgive me." The man made a dismissive gesture, and kept eating. I found myself in awe of their resilience.

Xad and Bane returned to our makeshift campground carefully carrying what looked like stone bowls filled with water.

"You found those?" I asked.

"No," Xad replied. "We made them." I blinked in

surprise. Upon closer inspection, the stone bowls had telltale carving marks.

"I'm impressed," I said. The pair grinned.

"We made the stone thin enough so that it will boil quickly," Bane explained. He collected a few sticks and some thin, sinewy vines, and used them to suspend the stone bowls half a foot off the ground. Xad collected dried leaves and dead twigs to place under the suspended stone bowls. He used a portable igniter to start a small fire. Bane brought over a few more empty stone bowls.

"Once it's boiled, we'll pour them in here so the water will cool faster," he said. The ground teams went through more extensive survival training than the strike teams, no wonder this seemed like second nature to them. I couldn't remember the last time I needed to rely on such skills. I realized how cushy my life as a general seemed next to these two.

The three of us took turns taking the bowls back to the nearby stream and refilling them. By the time we had enough water to go around, it was nearly nightfall. We would have to sleep here tonight and walk towards Glymna in the morning.

Surely my crew would be searching for us. The best thing we could do would be make it easy for them to find us.

I didn't relish the idea of sleeping out in the open

like this, but there was no choice. The humans needed rest before taking on such a walk. Luckily, the forest had been quiet. The presence of the Xathi in the area must have driven away the indigenous lifeforms.

Odd thing, to have something to be grateful to the bugs for.

I offered to take first watch. Now that the busy work of setting up camp had been completed, there was nothing to distract me from my thoughts of Vidia.

Every word she'd spoken was a blow. I should have said something to her, should have reassured her... but how?

We both had our duties.

But for the first time, I'd wanted to deny mine, to promise I could stay with her, here.

We could make a life together.

"General?"

Xad called softly. My watch was over, his had begun.

"My thanks, Xad."

And with that one word, reality crashed back in.

My duty could never be forgotten. Not as long as the men who'd sworn to fight at my side drew breath.

As I lay, staring at the canopy of green above, I plotted and schemed as hard as I ever had against an opponent.

This time, my enemy was time.

Before I knew it, the sun had risen. I hadn't gotten a wink of sleep.

The humans, on the other hand, had slept deeply. They were in a much better state than they had been the night before. The forest floor was littered with bits of discarded crystal.

I retrieved a few more fruits and berries for breakfast before we started our trek. Some of the humans were talkative and excited to have their bodies back. They spoke of their families, their friends, and all the things they were going to do now that they were free of the Xathi queen.

Others were quiet, still in shock over everything they'd gone through. One human didn't remember anything that had happened to her. The last thing she remembered was seeing her friend fall dead to the ground beside her. Perhaps it was a mercy she'd forgotten.

By mid-day, I was beginning to rethink my plan. We had to stop and rest often. Even the humans in the best condition tired quickly.

Then a sweet sound met our ears.

Bane looked to me for confirmation, and at my nod, ran off to a clearing through the trees, waving his arms like a madman.

Mad or not, it worked.

Within minutes, the shuttle had landed next to him, and my flock of humans had made it to the edge of the clearing, eyes wide. Tu'ver stepped out, swept the area, then came forward.

"We're happy to see you, General," he commented mildly.

"Not nearly as much as I am that you found us." While my tone was light, relief ran through my words. The humans would have made the trek.

Eventually.

And while I'd paid attention to Vidia and the doctors, three soldiers were no replacement for a town full of doctors.

"I'm afraid we're not going to all fit in there." The small shuttle was ideal for setting down in the dense vegetation, but it would take several trips to ferry everyone to Glymna.

"Just a moment, please." He stepped back inside, and when he reemerged, he was followed by Fen.

Who held the Gateway.

"Who authorized its removal from the *Aurora*?" I snapped.

Fen cocked her head, and touched her speech pad lightly. "I do not recall needing your authorization, General."

Of course she didn't. I scrubbed at my face. "My apologies. It has been a long night. If the Xathi--"

She made a fluid gesture towards Tu'ver. "I believe he's well equipped to handle that contingency. And we do want to get the survivors to medical attention as soon as possible, do we not?"

"You're right." I stepped away as she started to open a rift to Glymna. "It was good thinking. Thank you.'

Her hands busy with the Gateway, Tu'ver answered for her. "It was actually Vidia's plan. Smart lady."

Her name struck at me, made me want to urge Fen to hurry with the rift. Never had it seemed to take so long to open one.

But shortly, the way was clear and the survivors walked through, led by Xad and Bane. Tu'ver returned to the shuttle, and Fen stepped through with me, closing the rift behind us.

An enthusiastic group of volunteers, doctors, and even a few members of my own crew waited for us in the square... but I didn't see Vidia anywhere.

She still cared, she must, I reassured myself. But wouldn't Tu'ver have sent a comm that they'd found us?

Uncertainty gnawed, but I forced myself to wait until the last of the humans had been placed in the care of the doctors.

Finally freed, I searched for a familiar face, eventually finding Hannah, the daughter of Vidia's friend.

"Where's Vidia?" I asked immediately.

"She's on the *Aurora*." She looked worried. "I haven't seen her since you disappeared."

"Thank you."

I strode away, calling for Fen.

It was time to tell Vidia how I felt.

VIDIA

S till, no word.

The strike teams hadn't found Rouhr's body when they searched the area, so he hadn't been killed while fighting the Xathi.

Probably.

It was far too easy for my mind to play images of him, shot, wounded, torn apart by the Xathi, or dragged by the walking trees into a nest of giant spiders.

Clenching my fists until my nails cut half-moons into my palms, I tried to stop the barrage of images.

Rouhr was a fighter.

Vrexh and everyone else I'd met on the ship assured me he was a superb warrior.

He wouldn't be killed.

But that wasn't the only thing that could have happened, that could explain his absence.

My worst fear at that moment was that a Xathi had managed to grab him, knowing he was the one in charge, and dragged him away to the Xathi ship where the queen was waiting.

What would she do to him if she had him in her clutches? She wouldn't kill him. Not right away, at least. She'd try to look into his mind.

She could wipe us out in a day if she had the knowledge he possessed. She would know every weakness to hit, every nerve to pinch, every pressure-point to exploit.

She could try to turn him into a hybrid. His mind was strong. He would put up a valiant battle before succumbing to her power.

I knew Evie fought off the Xathi queen before, but she hadn't been on their ship. She'd been in a cabin under Sakev's watchful eye.

Rouhr would be tortured until he broke.

I shut my eyes, as if that would shut off the stream of thought. I had to stop thinking like that. It would only make things worse.

Evie had forced me back into my cabin on the *Aurora*, teasing that I'd drive the crew mad with worry if I didn't leave them alone for a bit.

It was probably teasing.

I might have been a little frantic, a little manic, coming up with ideas of places to search, ways to find him. She was right. The crew of the *Vengeance* were experienced, the Urai of the *Aurora* had unparalleled surveillance technology.

I should leave them to it.

But now that I was here, alone, with nothing to do but imagine every possible outcome, my body had locked, frozen, unable to keep up with the racing of my mind.

Until a battering at the door made me jolt.

"What?!" I shouted.

The knocking stopped abruptly.

Silence.

They'd found him.

They'd found his body.

And...

"Rouhr's back!" Evie shouted through the door. "Fen and Tu'ver found him, he went to Glymna, now he's back!"

I was out of bed in an instant. Spots swarmed my vision, and I had to steady myself against the wall.

"I'm coming!" My throat was sore, and I didn't even pause to put on proper clothing. I ran out of my room, barefoot, in a black tank top and the tiny, loose shorts I slept in most nights.

I opened my door and ran right past Evie, nearly

tripping over the untouched tray of food someone had left for me earlier that day. Evie yelled something after me that I didn't hear. I couldn't stop, I had to find Rouhr.

I tried to think of where he would go first after coming through the rift, but my brain couldn't focus on forming a single complete thought.

"Where are you? Where are you?" I muttered under my breath as I rushed around the ship. Everyone I passed probably thought I'd finally lost my mind. At this point, I'd say it was a definite possibility.

Rouhr wasn't in the main common area, the mess hall, or his office. Where the hell *was* he?

Had Evie been mistaken?

Oh, God, what if he was injured and bleeding to death in the med bay?

I took a deep breath and silenced my thoughts. As the doctor, Evie would've known if he was injured. She would've told me.

Unless that was what she had been trying to tell me when I rushed out of my room. I was about to turn around and ask her if he was hurt when the nearby elevator opened.

Rouhr rushed out, looking as frantic as I felt, uniform jacket in tatters, but whole.

Alive.

"Vidia!"

I ran to him, throwing my arms around his neck as he wrapped his around my waist.

"I'm sorry, I'm so sorry," I blubbered into his shoulder, "I can't help it. I'd rather have you for a little while than not have you at all."

He crushed me to him, breathing into the tangle of my hair. "I'm the one who's sorry. I never should have left you."

Suddenly he lifted me, and I wrapped my legs around his waist for balance. I leaned back until I could see his face.

"Are you sure you're alright? Should you be in the med bay? Should-"

"Vidia, hush." His lips crashed onto mine, stealing my breath with his unique, spicy taste. His tongue pierced my mouth, plunging and plundering until I gasped, limp in his arms.

He broke away, darkened eyes searching mine.

"Did you really just hush me?" I finally managed.

"It did seem effective."

"We need to talk," I managed, trying to wiggle out of his grip. For a moment, I slid further down his waist, until a broad hardness pressed into my core.

"Yes," he growled, "we do." He hoisted me back up, and my legs tightened around him instinctively.

The elevator chimed behind us and he walked on, ignoring the stares of the crewmembers. I buried my face in his chest, the flames of embarrassment doing nothing to distract me from that fleeting feel of him.

That had been him, his body, his... oh heck, right?

Could that even be possible?

Just for a minute, I kicked myself for not having a more detailed chat with Evie about how things worked with a Skotan, then the door opened, and Rouhr strode out into the corridor.

His hands pressed me to his body and suddenly, I couldn't get enough of the taste of his skin, peppering his scales through the tears in his jacket, thanking each one with a kiss for keeping him safe.

For bringing him home to me.

A low growl rumbled in his chest. "Vidia," he ground out. "We're almost to my cabin."

A small squeak escaped me as his hands tightened on my hips, and he groaned.

"You're not making this easier, love."

We might've passed people in the hallway, I didn't know.

Didn't care.

I hadn't had much time in my life for romance and for once I was grateful.

Right now, all I wanted was him.

All I would ever want would be him.

And as he stepped into his cabin and I heard the door close and lock behind us, my body felt like a live wire rubbing against him. Falling together, tangled in each other's arms on his mattress, the amber of his eyes was all I could see.

His hand slid under the hem of my tank top, then froze. "Vidia," he gasped, obviously struggling for control, "we need to talk. You're right, we should talk first."

I raised myself on one elbow to bite his neck. "No, we don't," I insisted. "Later. Right now, this may be all we have."

I bit harder, arcing against him as his nails grazed my side.

Tugging me upright for a moment, he pulled my tank off, tossing it into a corner of his room.

"So soft," he marveled, looking at the trail of red his nails had made on my skin. "So delicate."

With each lick, with each touch, he came closer to my breasts.

I squirmed, desperate for his touch, for the teasing to be over.

"I don't know," I gasped, incoherence growing, "if you know, or if Skotan women are built this way…"

The tips of his fingers danced across the underside of my breasts, and I shivered. "Yes," I encouraged, "more of that."

Generals learned quickly, apparently.

In no time, he was alternating licking and sucking

my tight nipples, twirling at one while lightly pinching the other.

My breath caught, my cries higher and higher until suddenly, he stopped, looming over me.

"I want more," he demanded. "Everything."

But he didn't move and I realized that, despite the need in his voice, it was a question.

He wouldn't take, wouldn't force.

But I would give, willingly.

And whatever time we had left, I'd be damned if I regretted a moment of this.

I lifted my hips to push my sleep shorts down, kicking them off to join the discarded tank top.

He stared down as I stretched beneath his gaze.

"Everything. Yours," I offered.

Tearing off the shreds of his jacket, he fell on me as if he hadn't eaten the entire time he was missing, as if the taste of my skin was the only meal that would sate his hunger.

A trail of kisses traveled down my stomach, then he nipped at my inner thighs, pushing my knees up, spreading them wide open before him.

He waited, then blew a stream of hot air across my slick folds.

I reached for him, begging for the teasing to end, but his strength kept me pinned, at his mercy.

Another hot breath, another, and then a long, slow

lick against my core sent me screaming, fists pounding into the sheets.

"I like our differences," he muttered, then resumed his place between my thighs, licking and nipping, sucking, until I splintered, drowning in the unceasing waves of sensation.

He stopped, then crawled over me, wrapping one arm behind my shoulders while the other stayed between my legs, finger softly playing with my folds as the quakes slowly subsided.

"So beautiful," he said, and kissed me, sweetly at first, then with growing intensity, his tongue breaching the seal of my lips as his finger plunged inside me.

"So small," he muttered, and shook his head. "I'm not going to hurt you. I won't."

He would. He would when he left.

And that would be the only thing I would allow to break me.

"Don't you dare stop," I demanded, rocking my hips against him.

"Vidia," he groaned, as I sped the pace, daring him to match me. "I can deny you nothing."

So slowly, sweetly, he drove one finger, then another, into me until I shattered again on his hand.

ROUHR

In all my years of command, through every battle I'd faced, never had my nerves been keyed to such a pitch.

I gazed down upon her, her dark hair tangled over my pillows, her eyes heavy-lidded, as Vidia waited for me.

I kicked off my boots and stepped out of my uniform pants, hotly aware of our differences.

But surely this would work. Two of our Skotans had taken human mates.

My Vidia wouldn't be harmed.

I wouldn't allow it.

Her eyes widened as she saw me for the first time unclothed.

"Well," she swallowed, "this should be interesting."

"We don't have to do anything you don't want to," I insisted.

Having her in my bed, drawing sweet cries of release from her, had been more than I had ever dreamed of.

"But I certainly do want to," she smiled, then beckoned me back to bed.

"I think we should start like this," and she pulled me down to the bed until I lay next to her, then she pushed me onto my back.

My chest tightened, remembering our night together in Glymna, how desperately I'd wanted to touch her then.

Now she straddled me, rocking her hips, dragging her wetness back and forth across my hard length.

"Oh!" Her eyes fluttered as my ridges hit against that delicate nub I'd found at the top of her slit.

Grinning, I wrapped my hands around her hips, pulling her back and forth against me, her heat making my cock even stiffer.

"Rouhr," she gasped, breaths short and faint, "let me up a bit."

I released her and she raised on her knees above me, then reached down, drawing a hiss from me as soft fingers wrapped around me, positioning me below her.

So very slowly, she eased lower, my fingers tearing at the sheets, every ounce of control I'd ever learned now in play as I desperately fought not to grab her sweet curves and drag her down, thrust into her all at once.

Her sweet, tight heat was indescribable. Then she stopped and I bit back my groan of frustration.

Vidia raised herself, slid down a tiny bit more, up and down, lower and lower, until we were both shaking.

Now she breathed, running her hands across the planes of my chest, and, in one swift movement, dropped herself until I was fully sheathed inside her.

Her head flung back with a low cry and then a lifetime of discipline snapped.

Arm wrapped around her waist, I lifted her up, slamming her back down on me, driving into her until she trembled, my name a soft moan on her lips.

With a quick twist, I lifted her, rolling us over until she was pinned beneath me, her legs tossed over my arms as I cradled her shoulders, driving into her over and over until, with a final scream, she came again, her contractions driving me over the edge right behind her.

Exhausted, she sprawled under me, the last tiny quakes of pleasure running through her as I caressed her.

Mine.

My mate.

Somehow, we would find a way to make this work.

"WE HAVE A PROBLEM." Evie burst into my office without knocking. Vidia and I were sitting together reading update reports on Glymna. Each day, more and more people were approved to be moved to one of the safe zones Evie had set up.

A setback, one that Thribb insisted was minor, had delayed the test flight of the *Aurora*.

Any day now, he maintained.

And Vidia and I would take all of them, until whatever the end would bring.

"What's the matter?" Vidia asked.

"The Xathi figured out how to breach the sonic barriers around the safe towns."

I was on my feet immediately. "How serious is it?" I demanded.

"It's under control, for now. When Fen set up the sonic barriers, she also set up an alarm that would sound if they ever malfunctioned," she explained. "As soon as the alarm went off, Sakev mobilized a team to get out there and deal with the Xathi."

"Any casualties?" Vidia asked.

"Thankfully, none," Evie sighed with relief. "The towns were prepared in case the barriers were compromised. The one that was attacked had safety bunkers that kept the Xathi at bay long enough for Sakev and his team to get there through a rift."

"Is the barrier still down?" I asked.

"As soon as the Xathi were taken care of, Fen and her team went out there and fixed it," Evie explained. "It's up and running now, but I have every reason to suspect the Xathi will try again."

"Right," I nodded in agreement. "Now they all know how to get around the sonic barriers, there's no reason they wouldn't try. How did they get through?"

"They figured out it was the sonic spikes that generated the frequency," Evie explained. "They gathered as close as they could without the barrier affecting them, and hit it with their neural whips until one shattered. It only took out a section of the barrier, but that's all they needed."

I clasped my hands behind my back, and paced the room. "All right," I sighed. "The Xathi know how to get past the barriers. They must suspect there aren't enough of us to guard every safe town at the same time. We can stop them and erect new barriers fairly quickly, but the Xathi won't desist with their attacks, especially if they believe they can wear us down."

"If they're smart, they'll organize multiple attacks at once. There's no way we can keep up with that," Evie answered, shoulders sagging. "We can't even risk putting up barriers at new towns. They'll know to attack before the barriers are complete."

"Even if they don't, we can't risk letting them figure it out," I replied. "Preventative measures aren't going to be enough anymore. We need to do something drastic."

"And fast," Vidia spoke up. "Glymna is starting to feel the strain from all of those extra people. They have to be relocated soon."

"A face-to-face battle against the Xathi is too risky in our current situation," I said. "Their ship is well-fortified. An aerial attack with our smaller vessels would be like throwing pebbles at a mountain, and a ground team stands little chance of a successful attack against it."

"Axtin managed it," Vidia offered.

"Yes, but he was lucky not to incur considerable casualties. It's not something I'd want to repeat, unless we had no other options," I replied. "Our best option is to cull the Xathi population to a manageable level. Only then could we consider attacking the ship."

"Then our only option is to lure the Xathi out," Vidia said.

"They're already attracted to the safe towns," I said. "We could fake a sonic barrier malfunction and draw a large group of them there and attack."

"Out of the question," Vidia responded before I'd even finished my sentence. "The people living in those towns have been through enough. I'm not asking any of them to play host to a battle against the Xathi."

"And the Xathi already know they don't need an army to overtake one of the towns. The citizens living there are basically defenseless except for their safety bunkers," Evie added.

"What's something the Xathi want more than the people?" Vidia asked.

"They took the minds of as many people as they could in an attempt to find the Gateway," Evie replied.

"We can't risk the Xathi getting that," Vidia shook her head.

"No, we can't," I agreed. "But if we can trick them into thinking we're taking the Gateway somewhere *other* than the *Aurora*, they'll surely come after us."

"But where would we possibly take it?" Evie asked.

"What about the *Vengeance*?" Vidia suggested. I stopped pacing to turn and look at her.

"The *Vengeance*," I repeated. Vidia nodded.

"We theorized that the Xathi set up a hybrid camp near the *Vengeance* just in case we ever returned. It's not far-fetched to assume they'll attack it again if they thought we were going back to it," Vidia explained.

"It makes sense," Evie agreed.

"Okay, say we convince the Xathi we're transporting the Gateway to the *Vengeance*," I speculated. "What advantages do we have if we choose to fight them there?"

"It's on our turf," Evie replied.

"We'll have access to the ammo that was left behind," Vidia added.

"Both good points, but you're forgetting something," I said. "The Xathi already overwhelmed us on the *Vengeance* once before. We know we can't take them in a fight head-on."

"We weren't prepared that time," Vidia argued. "This time, we'll know they're coming, and prepare accordingly."

"I think we should look for a better option," I said. "We could go into the fight well-prepared, but we'd lose more soldiers. We need to think of something that minimizes casualties on our side while maximizing casualties on their side, especially if our end goal is going to be a full assault on the Xathi ship."

"I think we need second opinions," Vidia ventured.

"I agree," I replied. I walked to the intercom on the wall, and summoned Axtin, Tu'ver and Vrehx to my office. Vrehx and Tu'ver were the best strategists on the ship. Axtin, as Vidia had said, had managed a direct attack on the Xathi ship. I wanted to hear his take on all of this.

All three arrived in my office within a few minutes. I

gave them a quick rundown of what we'd been discussing.

"We need to cripple the Xathi's numbers and dissuade them from attacking the safe towns in one fell swoop, while also minimizing casualties on our side," I summarized at the end.

"If you want to minimize casualties," Tu'ver began, "I would form a plan that doesn't call for hand-to-hand combat."

"How is that avoidable?" Axtin asked. "I agree that trying to fight them on the *Vengeance* isn't a good idea, but I don't see how we can eliminate all fighting."

"We don't need to fight them!" Vidia said suddenly. All heads turned to look at her. "We can set a trap," she explained.

"A trap?" Vrehx repeated, testing out the idea.

"It would guarantee no casualties on our side," I grinned.

"What kind of trap could we set that's big enough to take out an entire army?" Evie wondered.

"One of the towns?" Tu'ver suggested.

"Vidia already shut that idea down," I told him. "And she's right. It's not fair to put people who are trying to recover into a situation like that."

"We have some powerful explosives in our arsenal," Vrehx offered. "We could plant them somewhere, and set them off remotely from the safety of the *Aurora*."

"If we make the explosion big enough, lure enough of them in, we could kill a large portion of their army." I rubbed my chin. "When the queen watches it happen through the eyes of her minions, she might panic enough to insist that the remaining Xathi dedicate their efforts to guarding her. Without the hybrids, that would relieve the pressure on the towns."

"I'd really like to scare the shit out of the Xathi queen." A sadistic grin bloomed on Evie's face.

"Same here," Vidia replied.

"Where should we place the bombs?" Tu'ver asked, redirecting the conversation back to the main objective.

"The explosion needs to be huge, so it can't be anywhere near a civilian population," Axtin said.

"I think we already have our answer," Vidia said in a soft voice, refusing to meet my eyes.

"What do you mean?" Her tone worried me.

"We already discussed the likelihood of the Xathi believing we'd return to the *Vengeance*," she began, then trailed away.

"We agreed the *Vengeance* wasn't viable for this plan."

I knew where she was going with this, but for a moment, just a moment, didn't want to accept it.

"For a fight, but not as a trap," Axtin jumped in. "Look, I hate the idea as much as any one of us would, but you have to admit, it's a solid plan."

"The Xathi would never expect us to blow up our own ship," Tu'ver added.

"The *Vengeance* is half-buried in the ground," Vrehx added. "There's no way she'll ever fly again."

"You're right," I let out a deep sigh. I couldn't think of an argument against it, nor think of a better plan.

"We'll blow up the *Vengeance*."

VIDIA

"I'm not sure how comfortable I am with this," I said for the fifth time that hour.

Rouhr gave me an indulgent look, but I could tell he was trying not to roll his eyes.

"Nothing is going to happen to me," he assured me. "Unless, of course, I drop one of the explosives and detonate it by mistake."

"That's not funny!" I gently shoved his shoulder, hiding my own laughter.

"I know. I'm sorry! I couldn't resist." He raised his hands in surrender.

"It's not unreasonable for me to be worried after what happened on the last cure strike," I replied. "You were gone for almost two days!"

"That's a fair point," Rouhr nodded. "But, this time, a

Xathi won't destroy my comm, you'll be able to see me the whole time on the *Vengeance's* surveillance cameras, and Strike Team One will be with me."

"I'm glad they'll be there to keep you in line." I smiled wryly.

"Me, too," Rouhr chuckled. "Speaking of them, Vrehx and Tu'ver should be just about done prepping the explosives."

"I'll go to the control room, and make sure everything works properly," I offered. Rouhr smiled and kissed my forehead before leaving to meet up with Strike Team One. The moment he was out of sight, a hard lump formed in my stomach.

Logically, I knew this mission was far less risky than the cure strikes. But I'd already felt the cold, heart-stopping terror of thinking I'd lost him once.

It had felt like my heart had been cleaved right out of my chest.

I never wanted to feel anything like that ever again.

Not until... I pushed the thought away and made my way to the control room, where Fen was already waiting with the Gateway.

The monitors on the wall were tapped into the cameras mounted all over the *Vengeance*. It looked like most of the screens had survived the last Xathi attack, though some flickered to static every so often.

Fen had gone ahead and fetched a comm for me to use. I placed the cuff over my ear to test it.

"Rouhr, can you hear me?" I asked.

"Loud and clear." I could hear the smile in his voice. When Fen clicked onto our frequency, Rouhr asked her to open a rift. From where she was in the control room, Fen opened a rift a few feet in front of Rouhr and Strike Team One leading to the docking bay on the *Vengeance*.

"You're getting really good at that," I marveled. "It must be cool to be the gatekeeper of all space."

"I had not thought of it that way." I saw the humor in Fen's eyes. "Perhaps I should have a new title."

Once Rouhr and the strike team were through, Fen closed the rift and I turned my attention to the monitors to see where they now stood in the destroyed docking bay.

"Let's split up, and grab anything useful," Rouhr ordered.

"If the Xathi left anything good behind, that is," Sakev added.

Axtin went to the armory, Tu'ver stayed in the docking bay and started picking through the overturned equipment. Vrehx and Daxion went down to the engineering room and repair stations. Sakev decided to go to the med bay, likely at Evie's suggestion.

"Clipping an explosive to the power core will make a bigger explosion," Vrehx said through the comm.

"And one on the engine, too," Daxion added.

"Clip one anywhere on major gas lines, as well," Rouhr instructed.

Rouhr had gone to the main common areas of the ship, hunting for any useful everyday supplies to take back.

"I'll handle planting the explosives," Axtin offered. "There's nothing good left in the armory."

"Noted," Rouhr replied.

"The Xathi took most of our ammo," Vrehx called in. "It looks like they tried to take pieces of the ship, too, but stopped halfway through dismantling it."

Rouhr made his way to the bridge and central communication station. The Xathi had done a number on the ship's control panels.

"The Xathi really wanted to make sure we couldn't leave," Rouhr chuckled dryly. "As if being a quarter-buried in the center of a forest of walking death traps wasn't enough to stop us."

I took a closer look at the communication center on my monitor.

"Something's off about what they did," I murmured to myself.

"What do you mean?" he asked.

The cameras gave me an aerial view of the room. "They've destroyed every panel and board, but one." Near the front, opposite where Rouhr was positioned, one of the control panels looked like it'd been left untouched.

Rouhr approached, and carefully examined it.

"It's the local communication panel," he explained. "It's how I used to receive reports, help signals, and updates from other locations on the same planet."

"Why would they leave that untouched?" I asked.

"I don't know." Rouhr rubbed the back of his neck. "Unless…" he trailed off as he bent down to look underneath the tabletop, where everything connected. "Figures," he huffed after a few moments of silence.

"What?" I asked.

"The Xathi have tapped into our local communication lines." He straightened back up. "There's a crystal node right at the base of the transmitter."

"I guess that proves the theory of why they set up a hybrid camp so close to the ship," I replied. "But I wonder if we can make this work to our advantage."

"Tell me more, my clever girl," Rouhr bent down to examine the node once more while I was thankful the rest of his team couldn't see me blush.

"If it's on the transmitter, I assume they could hear all outgoing messages?" I ventured.

"Yes," Rouhr confirmed.

"And it wouldn't be a stretch to assume they could also hear any incoming messages?"

"Most likely," Rouhr replied.

"Fen was originally going to attempt to breach their communication center to plant a false message about the Gateway," I continued. "But it looks like the Xathi have left a breach for us."

"Using their own tech against them? I like it," Sakev laughed.

"There's a chance this Xathi ship's communication system could be entirely unfamiliar to me." Fen added. "They change their tech frequently, depending on which races they've overtaken. We can record the conversation over the comms, then I can release it to the compromised communications board. The Xathi will do the hard work for us."

"That settles that!" I said cheerfully. "Rouhr, are you ready to do a little acting?"

"Excuse me?" Rouhr blurted.

"Make sure to deliver a quality performance, General," Sakev quipped.

Rouhr rolled his eyes so hard I could see it on the monitor.

"Just try to sound natural," I laughed. "I'll start, and you can just follow my lead."

"General, the Gateway and the refugees are ready to be transported back to the *Vengeance*. Is everything all set on your end?" It felt strange calling Rouhr "General", but other than that, I did my best to sound as natural and professional as possible.

"The Xathi did some real damage," Rouhr sighed. "But the refugee bay is still mostly intact. How many are you sending over?" Rouhr was better at this than I'd expected him to be.

"A few hundred refugees, plus half the crew," I continued. "I want to move some of the cured humans to the *Vengeance,* as well. We've just got too many people to handle."

"Noted. We're ready when you are," Rouhr concluded.

"Opening a rift and sending them through now," I finished.

Fen stopped recording.

"Looks like we know what Rouhr's going to do when the war is over," Dax joked.

"Very convincing, General," Vrehx added.

"Don't bother sucking up to me. Flattery will get you nowhere," Rouhr chuckled.

"It was worth a shot," Dax replied.

"I think it'll work," I chimed in. "Fen and I will clean it up and prepare it for transmission while you finish planting the explosives."

"Right," Rouhr agreed. "How's it coming, Axtin?"

"Just planted the last one on the main gas pipe," he replied.

"Excellent," Rouhr said. "Is anyone near the power core?"

"I am," Vrehx replied.

"Go ahead and power up the *Vengeance*," Rouhr ordered. A few seconds later, I heard the *Vengeance* hum to life through the comm.

"If we change this strip of code right here," Fen pointed to a row of unintelligible characters on her personal monitor, "it will look like Rouhr's parts came from the *Vengeance* instead of the comms."

"That's amazing," I gasped then watched Fen make rapid adjustments to the audio files.

"That should do it," she said after a few moments.

"Perfect," I beamed. "Rouhr, as soon as the explosives are set up, you can come back to the *Aurora*. The transmission is ready when you are."

Rouhr didn't answer me right away. He'd moved from where I last saw him in the communication center. He was now on the bridge, gazing at everything with a faraway look in his eyes.

Of course.

That was his ship.

I put my comm to the side to let Rouhr say his goodbye.

ROUHR

Vidia was on standby, ready to send the message to the Xathi that we had returned to the *Vengeance.*

Time was of the essence, but I needed a moment to say goodbye to my ship.

"Just give me a few minutes," I asked Vidia.

"Of course," she replied.

I don't know if she understood anything about the bond between a general and his ship, but she was trying to.

That meant a great deal to me.

Truth be told, I'd never thought I would make it to general. I assumed I would be a rank and file soldier for the duration of my career on the force. I'd stayed in the ranks for fifteen years, longer than many of my people spent in service before the Xathi came.

I found being a soldier easy. All I needed to do was trust my leaders and follow orders, and that's exactly what I did.

I was the standard every soldier wanted to meet, but few did. There were others more skilled in battle than I, but I had an endless supply of resilience.

No matter how difficult the battle was, no matter how many of our crew were cut down, I pushed on. I would follow orders, and complete the objective no matter the cost.

I rose in rank quickly after becoming a commanding officer. The higher-ups realized early on that I was more qualified than most due to my long stint in the force.

Within four years, I had become a general, one of the youngest to do so. And when the hostilities with the Xathi boiled over, I was given command of my own ship, the *Vengeance*.

She wasn't the prettiest ship out there, but she was mine. I was given the freedom to govern my crew how I saw fit.

Up until recently, I would have given anything to go back in time and stop the experimental weapon that caused all this from ever getting put on my ship.

Now, despite all the death, destruction, and

sacrifices that had already happened and were still to come, I wouldn't go back.

I wouldn't trade my time with Vidia for anything.

Not even my beloved ship.

"It was an honor flying with you." I rested my hand against the main control panel where I had so often stood.

It took doing the right thing to acquire this honor.

Now, doing the right thing would cost me my ship, the command I'd fought hard to be worthy of.

The older I got, the more I noticed how funny life was.

"Rouhr? Are you okay?" Vidia's soft voice crackled through my comm.

"Yes," I replied. "I'll gather the men and call for a rift."

"Okay." I could hear the concern in her voice. I knew if there was any other option, Vidia would help find it.

But there wasn't.

"Meet back in the old docking bay for departure," I ordered. The men echoed their confirmations as I walked out of the bridge for the last time.

"I hope you've all said your goodbyes."

They nodded solemnly. The *Vengeance* had been their home, too. With a heavy hand, I lifted my comm and called for Fen to open a rift. When it opened, I was the last to go through.

The last to leave, as it should be.

Vidia and Fen waited in the control room of the *Aurora*.

"Hey," Vidia said with a soft smile as I walked in the door. I tried to smile back, but I don't think she was convinced. She slipped her arm through mine when I stepped up to the control panel and leaned her head against my shoulder. I kissed her hair, breathing in the sweet, clean smell of her.

"Are we ready to send the transmission?" Fen asked.

I nodded, then listened to the recording, my mind still far away, on the bridge of the *Vengeance*.

Vidia did excellent work. Her voice sounded calm, casual, and official. The Xathi would have no reason to suspect it was all a fabrication.

"Now we wait," I said.

There was nothing more to do except watch the monitors for signs of Xathi movement. Fen programmed one of her satellites to scan for living things of similar size and body temperature as the Xathi.

Almost immediately, there was activity around the Xathi ship.

"Looks like they got the message." A satisfied smile

appeared on Vidia's face. "That's what they get for trying to listen in on our conversations."

"So, that's your breaking point?" I laughed. "Not the hybridism, not the destruction of your planet, but eavesdropping?"

"It's rude!"

We watched swarms of Xathi move from their ship in the direction of the *Vengeance*. As we'd hoped, the queen appeared to have directed a large portion of her remaining forces to investigate.

It showed how much they wanted us wiped off the face of this planet.

Good. That made it even.

It took them less than an hour to make the journey. Fen toggled on the surveillance cameras inside and around the *Vengeance*. The Xathi tore through the ship, demolishing everything that wasn't already destroyed.

I hated watching the Xathi defile my ship, but I would get my revenge soon enough.

"You should do it," Vidia said, handing me the remote to activate the bombs.

"Thank you," I acknowledged. If anyone was going to destroy the *Vengeance*, it would be me.

The Xathi continued to tear apart the ship searching for us, for the refugees. I watched, waiting for the perfect moment. I wanted as many as possible to be inside the ship when I activated the bomb.

At one point, there was a shift in their demeanor.

They realized the ship was empty.

On each of their faces, I saw the Xathi queen scramble to figure out what was going on.

The clicks of confusion turned into shrieks of outrage when they figured out they'd been tricked.

Good.

I wanted the queen to know she was stupid and arrogant enough to walk right into our trap. When she saw her minions get blasted to pieces, I wanted her to know that it was us who had done it to them.

I pressed the button.

There was a single beat where time seemed to stop entirely.

Then, there was nothing but blinding light. The *Vengeance* blasted apart from the inside. Fire swirled through the corridors, knocking out the surveillance cameras one by one.

I didn't need to see the Xathi writhing and burning to know we'd won.

I pressed the intercom button on the control panel.

"Attention, everyone." I heard my own voice echoing through the speakers around me. "The mission was a success." From farther down the halls of the *Aurora*, I could hear cheering. Vidia stood beside me, smiling up at me. I tucked her under my arm and pulled her close, but I couldn't bring myself to smile just yet.

VIDIA

After destroying the *Vengeance*, Rouhr wanted to go back to his office and get some work done. I let him go, knowing the loss of the *Vengeance* had taken a toll on him.

He kept to himself for the rest of the day. I wouldn't have been surprised if he stayed up all night in his office.

The following morning, I still hadn't heard from Rouhr, but I decided it was best not to push him. He would seek me out when he was ready.

While I waited, I decided to visit the labs to see Leena and Evie. Since the final cure strike, they'd been working on refining the production of the cure and documenting everything, so their work could be officially published.

When I entered the lab, I expected to see both of them working hard in a state of deep concentration.

Instead, I found them giggling over a lab table that looked like a painting project gone horribly wrong.

"What's going on?" I couldn't help but laugh. Evie had a huge blue splotch on her lab coat, and yellow splattered across her face.

Leena didn't look any better, with a red smear on her cheek and what looked like purple dust covering her front.

"We're trying to make makeup!" Evie declared through her laughter.

"What?" I exclaimed. "What for?"

"Mariella is throwing a party tonight," Leena explained. "Now that the hybrids are cured, and the Xathi's army has been crippled, we all figured the last stage is the final Xathi takedown. Mariella thought we should have a last hurrah."

"It sounds so bleak when you say it like that," I replied.

"'Last hurrah' isn't the right term," Leena amended. "I'm sure there will be many more hurrahs to come."

"So, you're trying to produce makeup to wear to the party." I filled in the rest, decided it was better not to wait for her to come up with a better phrase. "Wouldn't it be easier to ask Fen to open a rift to Glymna and go to a store?"

Evie snorted. "We tried. Even sent a comm over. Everyone is too busy for such 'frivolous' endeavors."

"It is a little frivolous," I admitted.

"Maybe, but after everything else we've whipped up out of nothing in this lab, lipstick shouldn't be that challenging!"

I didn't actually have a good answer for that.

"None of us have party clothes. Won't we look strange walking around all made up, but still in our work clothes?"

"I doubt the aliens will realize we don't have proper party attire," Leena snorted.

"Fair point," I allowed. "When's the party?"

"It's later tonight," Leena answered, frowning at another concoction. "It starts as soon as Snipes finishes making all the food. The Urai even have music!"

I'll admit, I was curious to know what Urai music sounded like.

"Let me see what you've come up with so far." I stepped closer to the messy lab table and looked at the shallow dishes filled with colorful powders, gels, and creams.

"I can't remember the last time I wore makeup," Evie sighed wistfully.

"I used to have a whole closet dedicated to party clothes," I admitted. As Mayor, I often went to upscale events with other city leaders to schmooze and make under-the-table deals.

"I miss my shoe collection," Leena sighed.

Between the fighting, the Xathi, and all of the destruction, it was easy to forget that all of us were women who still enjoyed feminine things.

It would be nice to go back to that for a few hours. And as much as I didn't want to think about it, Leena had a point. This could be our last hurrah. The final confrontation with the Xathi was coming.

I didn't know what Rouhr had planned, but I knew it wouldn't be without risk.

We played around in the lab for a few hours, making more of a mess than anything else, until we had a small collection of functional products.

I managed to make an exact replica of my favorite shade of lipstick. I was applying it when Mariella's voice came through the intercom.

"You guys, come to the mess hall!" she squealed with excitement. "Snipes is finished cooking. The party's starting!"

"Let's go," Evie urged.

"You guys, go ahead," I said. "I doubt Rouhr knows about the party. I'll go get him."

The pair nodded before bouncing away, giggles echoing down the corridor.

Rouhr's office was across the common space from

the mess hall, but, just as I had suspected, he was holed up, completely oblivious to everything.

I knocked on the door before entering.

"Hey, stranger," I said from the doorway.

Rouhr frowned. "What's on your mouth? It's bright red," he exclaimed. "Are you sick?"

"It's called makeup. It's like ceremonial paint for special occasions," I laughed. "Do you like it?"

"It's… intriguing," he grinned slowly. "Makes it hard to look away from your lips."

"I could cover you in kisses and the color would blend right in with your skin," I teased.

"Is that the special occasion?" he asked. "Did you paint yourself just to kiss me?"

"There's actually a party going on, not that you noticed," I teased.

"Is there?" Rouhr seemed genuinely surprised.

"In the mess hall. It was Mariella's idea. How about we go over together, and have a little fun?"

"I've got so much work to do," he sighed. "The repairs are complete. I'm waiting for the Urai to perform their inspection, so they can tell me what the *Aurora* is capable of. I still have to plan the final assault on the Xathi, too."

"How long have you been working on that?" I asked, looking over the stack of datapads.

"All day," he admitted.

"Then you need a break anyway." I grabbed Rouhr's hand and pulled on him until he rose from his desk. "You probably couldn't see the perfect plan if it stood up on your desk and bit you at this point."

"I'll go for a few minutes, but then I really need to get back to work," he insisted.

"You're starting to sound like me," I laughed.

The mess hall was packed with crew members and refugees. Snipes had whipped up a feast consisting of human food and food from all four alien species.

A few of the humans had tried to figure out how to make wine and beer in the refugee wing and were handing out those drinks, as well as alien spirits.

Tables had been pushed aside to make room for dancing, the Urai's music was blasting through the intercom speakers. It was livelier than I'd imagined it would be, but still, like nothing I'd ever heard before. I liked it immediately.

"Impressive." Rouhr took in the sight before him.

"Mariella works fast," I laughed. I spied her in the middle of the open space, dancing with an uncomfortable-looking Tu'ver.

"You got him out of the office!" Leena approached me from the left. By the way she spoke, I could tell she'd had a few drinks already.

"How's the wine?" I asked.

"Terrible. Stick to the alien stuff," she slurred. Axtin appeared at her side with an amused expression. He gingerly lifted the drink from her unsteady hand, and gave it to me.

"Drink it. You need it more than she does." He shook his head and wrapped his arm around her.

The cup was one-third-filled with bright green liquid that smelled like flowers. With a shrug, I took a long sip. It tasted better than it looked. I quickly finished the rest. When I looked around, everything in the room looked soft and glowing.

"That stuff is amazing," I gasped. "Rouhr, you've got to have some."

"I've had enough Marloch Extract to last me a lifetime," he laughed.

"You used to have fun, General?" Axtin teased.

"Let's just say not even Sakev would've been able to keep up with me in my wild days," Rouhr chuckled.

Axtin clapped him on the back before hurrying after Leena, who'd wandered back to the bar area.

"Those two have the right idea." Rouhr nodded at Jeneva and Vrehx who were sitting at a small table in the corner, eating food and people watching.

"You're no fun." I stuck my tongue out at Rouhr, who snorted in response.

"You know exactly how much fun I am," he

whispered in my ear. Goosebumps appeared on my arms and a shiver ran down my back.

"I think you need to refresh my memory."

"I will," he assured me, "after we spend some more time at this party you so desperately wanted me to attend."

"Fair enough," I nodded once before becoming distracted. "Look at all that food! Let's go get some." Rouhr tipped his head back and laughed. It was one of the best sounds in the world.

"Okay," he agreed, and let me lead him to the long table bending beneath the weight of so many dishes. Snipes stood behind the table, surveying his work.

"Snipes, you've outdone yourself!" I exclaimed.

"It's been a while since I've cooked a right proper feast," he declared proudly. "Help yourself to everything. Let me know if I got your traditional feast foods right."

I filled my plate with more than I could possibly eat, and then filled a second one. I wanted to try everything I'd never tried before, but I also couldn't resist the human classics like mac and cheese, and French fries.

"You're fun at parties," Rouhr laughed as we sat down to devour our spoils. I'd never tasted such amazing food in all my life.

"I'm fun all the time," I corrected between

mouthfuls. At some point, I'd secured myself another cup of Marloch Extract, and convinced Rouhr to have a cup, too.

One moment we were eating and laughing, the next, we were swaying on the dance floor, surrounded by all the friends we'd made. Evie looked like she was on the verge of falling asleep in Sakev's arms. Amira and Dax were surprisingly elegant dancers.

Rouhr brought me another cup of what I assumed was Marloch Extract. I gulped it down greedily, realizing too late that it was actually water.

"Trust me," Rouhr said. "Marloch is a monster to deal with in the morning. You're going to thank me."

Time seemed to fly by, yet simultaneously stand still. The party slowed down well after dark. Nearly all of the food had been eaten. Everyone was struggling to stay upright due to either exhaustion or drunkenness.

I had vague memories of Rouhr carrying me out of the mess hall and laying me down on his bed in his cabin. We kissed for hours. Or maybe it was only for a few moments. It was difficult to say for certain.

He was right. Marloch Extract was not to be trusted.

I clearly remembered him helping me out of my work clothes, and the cool, refreshing feeling of his sheets sliding against my bare skin.

Before I fell asleep, the last memory was of the

warmth of his body and the security of his arms around me when he climbed into bed beside me.

Strong.

Safe.

Mine.

For now.

ROUHR

It was almost impossible to drag myself out of my bed and away from Vidia's warmth.

But unfortunately, it was necessary.

I had asked the Urai to run their own reports on the *Aurora* now that she was fully repaired.

The plan was to compare their reports to Thribb's, and get their opinions on using the *Aurora* for space travel.

All of the Urai engineers gathered in my office to give me the final report on the *Aurora's* condition. At my request, Fen joined them as the Urai who'd spent the most time with my crew and the humans. I'd hoped in case of a language miscommunication, she'd be able to clarify things.

I should have known the miscommunication wouldn't have been on the Urai's side.

"That's completely ridiculous!" Thribb shouted at Fen.

"Do you disagree with their findings, Thribb?" I sighed.

"Absolutely!" Thribb exclaimed. "They are willfully ignoring the maximum thresholds their systems can be pushed to."

"I don't think the Urai would push their systems past what those can tolerate," I replied.

"No, they wouldn't!" Thribb cried. I hadn't anticipated that.

"Then...I'm not sure what the problem is," I said carefully. "I'm no engineer, but I'm fairly certain that's a good thing."

"You misunderstand me," Thribb pressed his long, narrow fingers against his temples. "It isn't that they're going over the ship's maximums, it's that they aren't even coming close."

"Is that so?" I looked at Fen.

"The *Aurora* potentially could handle the vacuum of space," Fen nodded, slowly. "However, once a certain amount of strain is put on our systems, specifically the life support system and the environmental regulatory system, the overall stability of the ship rapidly declines and the chance of total system failure increases."

"I see," I pressed my hands together. "What does that mean for us?"

"It means that, within the atmosphere of this planet, the *Aurora* will be able to function well for at least a few hours," Fen explained. "However, if the *Aurora* were to go into space for longer than a few minutes, the results could be disastrous."

"That's 'could be.' Not 'will be,'" Thribb argued. "This is the final leg of our mission on this planet. That deserves some level of risk!" Thribb slammed his hand down on my desk.

"Some risk, yes," Fen agreed. "Using the *Aurora* to go after the Xathi at all qualifies as a level of some risk. Using the *Aurora* for long-term space travel is too big of a risk."

"Preposterous," Thribb scoffed.

"Thribb," I warned. "The *Aurora* has been our home for some time now, but we have to remember that she doesn't belong to us. The *Aurora* belongs to the Urai, and if they say that prolonged exposure to the space vacuum isn't possible, then we have to respect that."

"What are you going to tell the crew?" Thribb asked, voice wavering. "How are you going to break it to them that they won't be going home on the *Aurora*?"

"I've been very upfront with my crew. They've known from the beginning that they shouldn't pin all their hopes on the *Aurora*," I answered.

"Yes, you did." Thribb had a shifty look in his eyes that I didn't like.

"What are you not telling me?" I demanded.

"My calculations predicted a much more positive outcome," Thribb started. "The crew often pestered me with questions. I saw no reason to lie to them."

Well. This certainly made sense.

The edge of insubordination running through my trusted soldiers, the unreasonable expectations that we'd be able to leave at any time, now I understood.

Thribb had been feeding a mutiny, and the bastard probably hadn't even realized it.

"You were out of line to disclose such information," I growled. "You've led the entire crew to believe the *Aurora* will be safe for space travel. I'm going to call a meeting, and you are going to be the one to tell them that it's not."

Thribb went pale, but he didn't argue.

And once the men knew, I'd need to find Vidia. One part of our uncertainty was over. My stomach clenched. But what would that mean for our future?

Within twenty minutes, every member of the strike teams, as well as the representatives from the ground teams, had gathered in the largest room the *Aurora* contained. I'd never seen Thribb look so nervous.

"Thank you all for attending this meeting on such

short notice," I began. "Thribb has news he thinks all of you should hear."

All eyes turned to Thribb.

"Ah, well," he cleared his throat. "You see, the repairs have been completed. Tests have been run. *Numerous* tests. The Urai and I have both run numerous tests." He was starting to ramble, a sheen of sweat on his forehead.

"Just say it." Rokul's voice was hard and cold.

"The *Aurora* is not fit for space travel."

The room was eerily silent, the faces of the crew turned to masks of sadness and rage.

I stepped in front of Thribb.

He might be a bastard, and I might sympathize with their urge to string him up, but we still needed him.

"Listen to me," I said calmly. "The *Aurora* will not be the ship to take you back to your homeworlds, but that doesn't mean we should lose all hope."

"Our homes are probably long gone anyway," Sk'lar sighed. "I hate to say it out loud, but it's the truth. We saw the devastation the Xathi brought before we fell through the rift. We've been fighting them for months on this planet, and it's only been a single ship. Imagine what an entire fleet of the bugs is capable of."

"Don't give up yet," I replied. "We have a fleet of our own out there, too. We can't do much in that fight, but there is something we can do. We can wipe out the

Xathi on Ankau. We can stop them from spreading through this corner of the universe," I continued. "I know I am asking a great deal, but we need to come up with a plan of attack to rid this planet of those vile beings for good."

"The *Aurora* is still mobile, right?"

I didn't expect Karzin to be the first to speak up. His gaze was empty as he stared at nothing. I knew the news was hard on him, but I also knew him to be an exceptional soldier even in the face of hardship.

"Yes," I nodded.

"The Xathi have sent out smaller transport units, but they have no idea the *Aurora* is functioning again," he continued. "Let's use that to our advantage."

"Excellent start," I offered him a respectful nod.

His chin dipped only slightly, expression still blank.

"But the *Aurora* doesn't have any weapons," Axtin chimed in. "We could give the Xathi a surprise, but not much of a fight."

"We could lure them into another trap," Tu'ver suggested.

"What trap is big enough to take down all of the Xathi and their ship?" Sakev asked.

One terrible option came to mind.

"Fen," I turned to her. "What would happen if a rift closed while someone was walking through it?"

"A rift is a doorway. When it closes, one part will be on one side, the other, on the other side," she explained.

"I think we just found our trap," my thoughts raced, walking through the steps. "We can use the *Aurora* to lure the Xathi into the air. Once they're following us, and I'm sure they will if they think we're trying to run, we can open a rift big enough for the Xathi ship to go through. Once they're right in the middle, we snap it closed."

Nods slowly rippled through the room as the men followed.

"Then, we open another rift, and return to the planet before the *Aurora* faces any complications," Tu'ver concluded.

"It's possible," Fen admitted, though I detected some uneasiness in her expression.

"I think it's our best shot," I replied.

"I agree," Vrehx added.

My crew echoed his sentiments unanimously.

I nodded with approval. "What can we do to make this easier on the *Aurora*?"

"If we can power down non-vital sections of the ship, that will make a great deal of difference," Fen replied. "And if we minimize the weight carried."

"Right," I nodded. "All civilians will be evacuated to Glymna for the duration of this mission," I announced. "That will be our first priority."

Vidia was not going to be happy about that.

"The rift is going to cut the Xathi ship in half, right?" Dax asked.

Fen confirmed with a nod.

"That means one half will be in space and the other will still be in this planet's atmosphere."

He raised a good point. I considered it for a moment.

"The *Aurora* will fly with a minimum crew," I decided. "Everyone else will be on the ground, prepared to deal with the fallout. We'll lead the Xathi away from any inhabited regions so nothing will fall on the cities and towns. If any Xathi survive the fall, they'll be bad off. Easy work."

The crew nodded.

"Let's set this in motion as soon as possible," I ordered. "There's no reason a single Xathi should still be alive on this planet by nightfall. Dismissed."

"General?" Thribb's voice sounded smaller than I'd ever heard it before.

"What, Thribb?" I asked.

"I've done the crew a disservice."

He at least had the guts to look me in the eye when he spoke.

"I wonder if you'll allow me to make up for it by lending my assistance on board the *Aurora* in this final stand against the Xathi."

"That's quite the offer," I said. "Are you certain? It'll be dangerous. I can't promise we'll survive it."

"I'm certain."

"Very well, Thribb. I'll let you know when we are to depart."

VIDIA

"I've been studying your idioms," Rouhr said, leaning against the doorway to my office, where I stared at the latest reports of towns that had applied to us for more protection from the Xathi.

"Seems like an interesting hobby," I smiled, happy to see him look relaxed, easy in his skin for the first time in days. Or scales, I supposed.

Either way.

"I've got good news, and bad news," he said, and my heart sank. "Or maybe it's bad news, good news, bad news. Maybe I haven't been studying as much as I thought I had."

"Well, then." I swallowed hard, my throat tight. "I've always wanted the bad news first. So, let's have it."

He stepped into the office, his face grim. "The

Aurora won't fly. Well, she will for short periods. But she won't ever be truly space worthy. The crew is trapped here."

My hands flew to my mouth. How could something that condemned so many lives to separation from their homes and families still make me so happy?

I was a terrible, selfish person, but still.

Fingers trembling, I reached for him. "And how do you feel about that?" I asked, quite proud of myself for keeping my voice level.

He grabbed my hand, then drew me around the desk and into his embrace. "Heartbroken for the crew members that wanted to go home, of course," he murmured, hands stroking down my back. "Conflicted, a bit, about how this affects the oath I swore to the Skotan fleet."

I closed my eyes, bracing myself.

His warm hand cupped my cheek, tilting my jaw up till I met his eyes.

"And immensely pleased that you and I will have a chance to see what develops between us."

His lips brushed over mine before he pulled back.

"That was the first of the bad news pieces, I suppose, wrapped with the good news."

I bit my lip. "You said there was another piece of bad news. Go on, tell me."

"We've come up with a way to defeat the Xathi," he

admitted, fingers kneading into my back. "But you're not going to like it."

At the very least, I was glad he gave me loads of work to do so I wouldn't lose myself in worry. Moving the refugees that had been with the crew since they were brought aboard the *Vengeance* was a strangely bittersweet experience.

Many refugees sought out crew members they wanted to say goodbye to, just in case something happened to them. All of the crew that wasn't going up in the *Aurora* was getting ready to load and go to their positions out in the desert. Even those with no formal combat training had a part to play.

Rouhr and I both had a lot of work to do over the next twenty-four hours. I knew we wouldn't get to spend as much time with each other as both of us wanted, so we had comms linked through a private frequency so we could talk as we worked.

That was probably for the best, anyway. If Rouhr saw what a nervous wreck I was, I knew it would be distracting for him. He had so much to think about, I didn't want to add to the load.

"How are the refugees taking the move?" he asked.

"They're far more sentimental about the ship than I

thought they'd be," I admitted. "The *Aurora* was a safe haven."

"I'm glad that's the case," he replied.

"How are the preparations on your end?" I asked.

"The Urai engineers are doing some last-minute tune-ups on the *Aurora* that will help her last in deep space a little bit longer," Rouhr explained. "The first transport units out to the desert just left. They aren't going as far out as Amira and Dax went, just far enough so that the cities are out of fallout range."

"I'm glad the majority of the crew will be out there. Any Xathi that manage to survive the fall through the rift won't stand a chance," I said.

"That's the idea," Rouhr agreed. "It might sound like overkill, but I think we're due for it."

"I couldn't agree more," I said.

"You know what I haven't been able to stop craving?" Rouhr said suddenly.

"What?" I asked, wondering where on earth this was going.

"Those long, thin things we ate at the party. Kind of a pale yellow? Crispy on the outside, soft on the inside. Salty."

"French fries?" I chuckled.

"Yes! Those things are a warrior's food, and delicious. I can't believe it took me that long to try them," Rouhr said enthusiastically.

"I know how to make them." I knew he was trying to distract me. It was a sweet gesture, and it really was helping ease the tight ball of worry in my chest.

"Why are you only telling me this now?" Rouhr demanded. "I would've started courting you much sooner if I'd known you could make such delicacies."

"You're ridiculous," I laughed.

"Anything to make you smile," he replied.

"Vidia." Evie rested a hand on my shoulder. "It's time to move the refugees to Glymna."

"Oh, fantastic," I said, though my voice fell flat. I grabbed a datapad with a long list of names. When refugees started arriving on the *Vengeance*, I had done my best to document them so they could be reunited with family and friends later on. When the Xathi attacked, and we had to relocate to the *Aurora*, I had lost all of that information. I'd started the process of collecting it again, but I didn't have anywhere near a complete list. My plan was to stand by the rift into Glymna, and take everyone's names manually. It was going to take a long time, but I needed a long distraction.

"Go get your work done," Rouhr urged. "I'll be around for a little while longer."

"Keep your comm on you," I replied.

"Of course," Rouhr assured me.

I made my way to Fen, who was waiting outside the

Aurora with the Gateway. Evie, Leena, and Mariella helped the refugees to form a line in front of where Fen would open the rift. I explained that I would need everyone's name before they passed into Glymna. Fen opened the rift, the first refugee stepped up, and the arduous process began.

Only one in every four refugees was already on my list. That just went to show how little progress I'd made in reclaiming my lost information. After over an hour of taking names with far too little progress, I enlisted the help of Amira and Jeneva. I gave them each datapads with the same list that I had, and asked Fen to open two more rifts. That sped up the process considerably.

We finished just before nightfall. When the last refugee went through the rift, I handed my datapad to Jeneva.

"I'll be back in a minute," I assured them. Before they could ask what I was doing, I ran back into the *Aurora*. Rouhr wasn't in his office. Instead, he was in the control room with Fen, learning as much as he could before it was time to lift off.

"Vidia, what are you doing here?" He was surprised, but not unhappy, to see me.

"I'm about to go to Glymna," I explained. "I just wanted to wish you luck." My voice broke on the last word. Rouhr walked over to me and wrapped me in his arms. Fen politely left the room to give us a moment.

"I'm glad you came to see me," he whispered.

"I couldn't leave without saying goodbye," I replied. He pulled away to look me in the eye.

"It's not goodbye," he said with a gentle smile. "By this time tomorrow, the planet will be Xathi-free, and we'll be sitting down to a nice, quiet dinner."

"Promise?" I asked.

"Promise."

Logically, I knew that, regardless of any promise, something could go wrong, and I could lose him. But hearing him promise to come back made me feel a little better about all of this.

I stood on my tiptoes to kiss him. He kissed me back hard, holding my body against his to the point where it was almost painful. After a few minutes of letting myself get lost in him, I pulled back.

"If you don't let me go now, you'll never get me off the ship," I warned. He laughed dryly.

"You're right," he nodded. "Get back to Glymna. I wager there are loads of people who could use your help." I hugged him one last time before walking out of the control room. It took all of my self-control not to run back to him.

I held in my tears until I was far away from the control room. I cried softly all the way back to the outside of the *Aurora*, where the rifts to Glymna were still open, waiting for me. I wiped my eyes and stepped through.

"You can close the rifts now, Fen," I called through the comm. The rift behind me disappeared. I found the other women immediately. They were all sitting together on a cluster of plush couches, looking as forlorn as I felt. I plopped down in the empty seat next to Evie.

"This sucks," Amira sighed. She passed me the datapad she'd been using. Jeneva handed hers to me, too, as well as the one I'd asked her to hold for me.

"Does anyone else feel like they're going to be sick?" Mariella's usually rosy complexion looked sallow.

"I feel like I'm going to pass out," Evie replied.

"We just have to remember that they're trained for this, and that they're the best at it," Jeneva said calmly, though her eyes were filled with tears.

"We should form a club," Leena said. I couldn't tell if she was joking or not. "We can meet up every time one of our men risks his life."

"So, daily meetings, then?" Amira replied. All of us giggled a little bit. We stayed up late, chatting long into the night about our mates, our worries, and our hopes for the future.

We must have fallen asleep right there on the couches, leaning against each other. The next thing I was aware of was being gently shaken awake by Seraphe.

"Hello, ladies," Seraphe spoke softly. Many of the refugees were still sleeping all around us on cots or soft mats. "I'm sorry to interrupt. I know you all must be feeling quite distressed." None of us answered her. "If I may, I'd like to offer you the use of our observatory. It's the finest on the planet. It will be your best chance to observe the *Aurora*, if you wish."

I brightened up immediately, as did the other women.

"Yes, please," Evie said, getting to her feet.

"Excellent! Follow me!" We hurried after Seraphe, who led us through the caverns of the city, up stairs carved into the side of the mountain, and over stone bridges until we must have been right under the mountain's peak.

Seraphe led us through a set of bleached stone doors into a circular room made completely of glass. The sky stretched out above us in shades of pale pink, yellow, and white. It must have been very early in the morning.

"I've already programmed it to the *Aurora's* coordinates," Seraphe explained. "Once the *Aurora* starts to move, you can track the ship here." She gestured to a gleaming control panel with knobs, buttons, and levers. "Don't worry about anything happening downstairs," she insisted. "My colleagues and I will take over for now."

"Thank you, Seraphe," I replied. I didn't risk saying anything else for fear that I would burst into tears.

"Of course, my dear." She patted me on the cheek lightly before leaving the observatory.

"Look!" Mariella said. "This will put whatever the telescope is seeing on the screen, so we can all watch." Mariella pressed a shiny button, and the large mounted monitor at the left side of the telescope flickered on.

At that moment, the *Aurora* was steadily lifting off the ground to align with an open rift. We grasped each other's hands as we watched the ship slide through and vanish.

ROUHR

It didn't take long for the Xathi to start firing at us, but it wasn't a problem for the agile *Aurora*. The skilled pilot, a Urai called Mar, effortlessly dodged the incoming projectiles.

The Xathi's guns were heavy hitters, but the downside to such big, powerful guns was the time it took to reload and re-aim. Mar ensured that we used that to our advantage.

However, we hadn't anticipated the Xathi's ship to lift off the ground as quickly as it did. Our plan was to badger them until they had no choice but to agree to an aerial fight.

Our mistake was assuming they wouldn't want to.

I should've guessed that after the *Vengeance*

explosion, the Xathi queen would be desperate and enraged enough to charge into a fight with us.

"Fen," I called to her. "Get ready to open the rift on my call."

"I will try," she replied. "But rifts of that size take time."

"Understood," I nodded. "Mar, keep the Xathi distracted until Fen has the rift open."

Mar didn't reply, but I knew that was because he was so focused on the *Aurora's* controls. He didn't want to risk breaking focus to use his speech pad.

The *Aurora* banked hard to the left around the side of the Xathi ship. Their guns never came close to us. I watched the Xathi struggle to orient their ship as we zipped under and around them.

As serious as this was, I couldn't help but revel in being back in the air.

We'd been grounded for far too long.

"How are we doing on that rift, Fen?" I asked.

"It would be done faster if I didn't have to answer your questions," she replied.

"Noted."

"Mar, keep heading out to the desert. We need to get as far away from the cities as possible."

The *Aurora* continued its evasive maneuvers in an eastbound direction. The Xathi ship continued its pursuit.

"The rift is open!" Fen reported. "We must hurry, it is very unstable."

An abrupt sound of metal striking metal rang through the control room. One of the Xathi's projectiles had skimmed the *Aurora's* hull.

"Thribb, damage report!" I called.

"No structural compromises," he reported back. "She's holding steady."

"Excellent." I switched the comm to the frequency of the ground teams below. "Ground teams, are you in position?"

"Yes, General," Vrehx replied.

"We're approaching the rift. Once we're on the other side, we will likely lose contact," I said. "Are you clear on your mission?"

"Yes, Sir," Vrehx confirmed.

"It's been a pleasure, Vrehx," I replied.

"We'll see you when this is over," he answered.

I laughed before clicking off the frequency.

"Approaching the rift," Fen reported.

"Let's do this," I nodded.

We neared the twisting gash in the sky. The *Aurora* abruptly turned upward, gathering speed until we passed through and found ourselves floating in the great expanse of space. Stars glittered against a velvet backdrop of sky.

I'd forgotten what a beautiful sight this was, the clean purity of space.

"Xathi incoming." Fen's voice jarred me back to the battle.

As the Xathi ship neared the rift, I wondered if the queen was aware of the danger she was in, or if revenge was all that mattered to her at this point.

"On my signal," I ordered. The Xathi ship began passing through, leaving Ankau.

One of the Xathi's guns hung out a little too far off the ship and snapped off where it came into contact with the rift. I waited until just under half of the Xathi ship was through before signaling Fen. "Close it up!"

"Hold on to something!" Fen ordered as she slammed her fingertips into specific points on the Gateway.

The rift shut like a vice. One moment, the Xathi ship was whole, the next it was cut clean in half.

The force of the rapid closure sent a shockwave through space, slamming into the half of the Xathi ship on this side of the rift, sending it spinning out of control, coming apart in a thousand pieces.

The shockwave slammed us, too.

We spiraled into deep space, hammered by fragments of the enemy ship.

Mar was able to get the *Aurora* under control quickly, and I was grateful for it.

"Fen, how much time until the *Aurora's* systems are overburdened?"

"Approximately one minute and twenty-three seconds," she replied.

"Go ahead and open a rift back to Ankau," I said. "Take it easy this time, we don't want another shockwave knocking us off course."

"Yes, General."

I turned back to watch the Xathi ship float lifelessly through space. Some of the Xathi had fallen out and now tumbled through the vacuum. Some were still twitching. I wondered if the queen was out there, floating lifeless among the stars.

A sharp clatter sounded behind me.

I spun to see Fen crumble silently to the deck, the Gateway rolling away from her limp hands.

"Fen?"

A clatter rattled through the control room as a short blade coated in blue blood dropped to the deck.

Thribb grabbed the Gateway, pressing at it, poking and prodding frantically at the lit sections. "This is our chance, don't you see?" His voice was high and pinched. "I couldn't let her take our chance away."

At his feet, Fen's arm moved, her dark eyes blinked slowly.

"Fen, are you all right?" It felt like such a stupid question. Her hand moved toward her speech pad.

"I will survive," she said. "Get the Gateway."

"No!" Thribb snarled. "This is our chance."

"Chance for what?" At the moment, he hadn't stumbled upon the way to open a rift, but at any moment he could get lucky. Keeping him distracted for now was our only chance.

But we didn't have long.

"To go home!" Thribb exclaimed. "We're off that wretched planet. We have the Gateway! We can escape!" His voice cracked.

"Thribb," I took a slow step toward him. "You know the *Aurora* can't last long in space. Give me the Gateway before it's too late."

"No! I can't turn my back on my world!" he screeched. "I'd rather destroy the Gateway before I let it come to that."

"Listen to me," I said gently. "I understand how difficult this is, but right now, we have to go back to Ankau."

"You just want to go back to your human whore! So many of you have been put under their spells! They've wanted us to suffer and bleed for them while our worlds burn."

Thribb had truly lost his mind. He didn't notice Fen sliding away toward the back of the control room. She pressed a small button under one of the countertops.

"Thribb, I need you to think carefully," I said. "Do

you remember why you joined the *Vengeance* crew?"

"Why are you stalling? We must escape now! My people need me," Thribb howled. He shook the Gateway, but it still refused to respond to his touch.

I took a deep breath.

Thribb was a Sugavian, the only one in the crew, and for a good reason.

For him, there was no world to go back to.

I wondered how long he'd been carrying these delusions. His fervent obsession with completing the *Aurora's* repairs finally made sense.

"I need you to answer the question," I replied.

"Enough of your questions!"

The rest of the Urai crew, aside from Mar, entered the room. Two of them went to assist Fen, the others took in the scene before them. "I did not spend weeks altering my calculations to fail now!"

"That sounds like a lot of work." And explained why the Urai's results were so different from Thribb's.

"Yes! I've been feeding you false calculations so we would have enough supplies to last us on our journey home!" Thribb exclaimed, as if his motives were logical. Obvious.

"Did you tell the crew we'd be able to go home on the *Aurora* on purpose?" I asked.

"I needed to ensure the others would be on my side when I realized you weren't going to listen to me."

Thribb's shrill laugh sent a shudder down my spine. On the control panel beside me, red lights started flashing.

The *Aurora's* systems were failing.

"I have to save my people!" Thribb shrieked over the cacophony.

"Your people are dead, Thribb!" I shouted, temper fraying. We were out of time. "Your planet was destroyed by the Xathi. That's why you joined my crew. Don't you remember?"

"You're wrong!" Thribb screamed. "You're a liar! You're a murderer!"

"Thribb, I'm so sorry."

I lunged at him before he could respond, and we hit the deck hard enough that his shoulder crunched underneath my weight.

The Gateway slipped from his grasp. Zan, the one who was with Amira when the Gateway was found, picked it up.

"Get us back, if you can," I ordered.

Thribb fought against me, but I had the advantage of size, strength, and experience. Still, madness drove him on.

"Thribb, you need to stop struggling this instant." I tightened my grip on him until he could barely move. "I don't want to hurt you."

"You're killing my people," he rasped.

"We've all suffered great losses at the hands of the

Xathi," I said. "There's nothing more we can do for our homeworlds. We have to carry on."

The *Aurora* began to move once more. I assumed Zan had successfully opened a rift.

Something in Thribb seemed to snap into place. His eyes went dull, that manic spark gone.

"I've made a grave mistake," he said softly.

"We're going to get you some help when we land, understood?" I said.

He nodded. I released my grip on him, and helped him to his feet. "Put him somewhere where he won't harm himself or others," I instructed one of the Urai crew members, who led him away by his arm.

Fen was back on her feet. The other Urai had patched her up enough to stop the bleeding.

"I apologize for allowing him into the ship," I said. "I should've known he was unstable."

"War changes all of us," was all she said.

As we approached the rift, the *Aurora* suddenly shuddered and groaned.

"What was that?" I demanded.

"System failure, as I feared," Fen said. She rushed to the control panel as quickly as her injury would allow. She started pressing buttons and flipping switches faster than I could comprehend.

"Prepare for a crash landing," she said to me as we started freefalling through the rift.

VIDIA

"Holy shit, they actually did it!" Amira squealed. She and Jeneva wrapped their arms around each other, and jumped up and down as chunks of debris tumbled from the sky into the desert. Mariella cried tears of relief. It was over.

We had our planet back from the Xathi.

But still...

"Why haven't they come back through?" I asked after nearly two minutes had passed.

Fen had warned Rouhr that the *Aurora* couldn't survive long in deep space.

Immediately, my head swarmed with visions of everything that could've possibly gone wrong. They could've collided with a chunk of the Xathi ship. The

Aurora's systems could've failed immediately upon entering deep space. The hull's structural integrity might not have been as stable as they thought it was.

I couldn't panic. If I did, I would come apart completely. I took slow, deep breaths, trying to steady my racing heart. I put my hands on my hips, and it was then that I remembered I never took my comm off.

I flicked it to the private frequency I'd shared with Rouhr, but that channel was nothing but static.

I flipped through the frequencies until I heard voices. I recognized the voices of the strike team members amidst the sounds of battle.

"Status report!" I demanded, startling the other women. "Anyone! I need a status report now."

"A large number of Xathi survived the fall from their ship." Tu'ver responded. As a sniper, he wouldn't be in the thick of battle. He'd be somewhere a little way off with a good vantage point. "Our soldiers and supplies are holding."

"But where is the *Aurora*?" I demanded.

A long pause. "No sign."

I looked at the timepiece in the observatory. Nearly four minutes had passed.

"What's happening?" Evie asked.

"Things are going well for the ground team," I said first, to give the other women peace of mind about their mates. "But there's no sign of the *Aurora*."

My throat thickened with emotion. I raised my hand to my chest as if that would stop my galloping heart.

"Vidia, you look pale," Evie said gently. "I think you should sit down." She reached for me so she could help me, but I shied away.

"No," I insisted. "I need to know where the *Aurora* is." I clicked back to the private frequency Rouhr and I were using.

"Rouhr? Can you hear me?" I shouted into the comm. The sound of snapping static was all I received in response. I clicked through the channels again. I knew Rouhr said that he would go out of contact when the *Aurora* was in deep space, but I had to keep trying.

Five minutes had passed since the *Aurora* went through the rift.

Something must have happened. As soon as the rift snapped on the Xathi ship, they would have been able to engage in combat.

Fen had mastered the Gateway at this point.

Opening a rift for the *Aurora* to return should've been no problem.

Six minutes.

A shuddering sob racked my body as the cold reality of the situation settled around me. If the *Aurora's* systems hadn't failed yet, they soon would.

With each passing second, I lost hope that Rouhr would come back to me.

"Vidia." Evie gently rested her hand on my shoulder. That small bit of contact caused something to break within me. My legs began to wobble. Evie caught me as I slumped forward.

"He promised," I sobbed into her shoulder. "He promised he'd come back." Evie didn't say anything, simply rubbed my back and let me cry. The other women flocked around me, offering kind words and gentle hands.

"Wait, what's that?" Amira asked.

I lifted my head from Evie's shoulder and looked at the monitor. I didn't see the *Aurora*, but I did see a new rift. I wiped the tears from my eyes, clearing my vision.

"They must be alive," Leena whispered.

"Then, where's the ship?" Jeneva whispered back.

"Please," I begged quietly. "Please, come home to me."

The *Aurora* came through the rift, bow first. I noticed something was wrong when the hull came into contact with the edge of the rift and bits of metal flew off like paper scraps. As they fell through, the bow didn't pull up.

The *Aurora* plummeted toward the planet's surface.

"I think their systems failed," I gasped. I reached for

the comm again, and clicked to the frequency the ground team was on.

"What's happening?" I demanded.

"The *Aurora's* engines aren't responding," Tu'ver replied.

"What the fuck are they going to do?" I demanded.

"The *Aurora* has an emergency landing system," Tu'ver explained. "It can redirect air currents to level the ship for a smoother crash landing even if there's no power to the engines."

"Why aren't they doing that?" I could hear my voice growing frantic and shrill.

Tu'ver remained silent, but I knew what he must be thinking. He thought most, if not all of them, were dead or incapacitated in some way.

I refused to believe that. Someone had opened the rift.

Someone must be fighting to save the *Aurora*.

"What can you see?" I asked Tu'ver.

"Not much," he said honestly. "But a gust of wind tipped the bow up and leveled the ship a bit. I think that's what they needed to jumpstart the emergency landing system."

I clicked to the private channel, holding my breath until I heard something other than static feedback. It sounded like blaring alarms and whooshing air. It had to be Rouhr's comm on the *Aurora*.

"Rouhr? Are you there?" I screamed. No response.

"He probably can't answer if he's performing the emergency landing," Evie reasoned.

I nodded and forced myself to breathe. I hoped that was the case. I couldn't bear it if it wasn't.

I couldn't hear anything but the alarms and the wind. I told myself that no one was loud enough to speak over something like that.

"Rouhr," I began again. "I don't know if you can hear this. If you can, you don't need to answer me. Just listen. You are the strongest, kindest, most incredible person I've ever met. My life would be empty without you. I love you more than anything. Please come home to me."

I set the comm on one of the countertops. The six of us stood close together as we listened to the static and watched the monitor. Every time the ship leveled out, we tried to figure out if the wind currents had been purposely redirected or if it was just a coincidence. Before long, the *Aurora* dipped below the curvature of the planet, and we lost sight of her.

On the comm, there was a horrible crashing sound. So many loud noises happened at once that it all blended together into one deafening roar. I squeezed Evie's hand and waited for silence to fall.

Once it did, I wished for the roaring again.

The silence was unbearable.

There were faint rustling sounds. It was hard to tell if it was someone's movement or the ship settling. The rustling grew louder until it sounded like something was brushing up directly against the comm.

"Vidia?"

EPILOGUE: VIDIA

The last few months had been....well, not quiet. But the scars across our planet showed signs of healing.

There was no point in moving the *Aurora*, not when we had the Gateway.

Besides, I never liked the swamp lands. I was much more suited for the desert. After spending the majority of the past few months either within a spaceship or inside a city built into a mountain, I was ready for some light.

I made time to stretch out on a blanket under the desert sun. My skin was on its way to becoming the rich golden shade it once was.

Sometimes Evie or Leena would join me, but most of the time, I was alone, with nothing but a datapad filled with fiction to keep me company. It was my little treat to myself for working my ass off.

That was one of the things Rouhr and I had agreed to work on. It was perfectly fine for us to love our work, but we needed to stop loving it at the expense of ourselves or our relationship.

Now that the Xathi were gone and the planet was healing, we promised each other that we would start working at a reasonable hour, come home at a reasonable hour, and get at least six hours of sleep a night. Eight was still too much to ask from either of us.

Besides, not all of that rack time was spent sleeping. There needed to be time for that, too.

Rouhr walked into our cabin, holding a steaming mug. I smelled the coffee instantly.

"Put that down!" I exclaimed.

"What?" The rim of the cup was already against his bottom lip.

"You're breaking one of the rules." I pointed an accusatory finger at him. "No coffee after sundown."

"But you said time doesn't exist," he argued.

"That was when I'd pulled a twenty-two-hour shift at the Glymna rehab center and you had to carry me home," I reminded him.

"Oh, that's right," Rouhr nodded. "You kept calling me a sexy red man."

"I most certainly did not!" I gasped.

"You most certainly did!" Rouhr was having trouble containing his laughter. His shoulders shook with the effort, causing him to slosh a little coffee over his hand. "Skrell!" He quickly set the mug down and shook the hot liquid from his skin.

"That's what you get." I stuck my tongue out at him. It was amazing how he could make me feel like a silly teenager in love for the first time.

Rouhr narrowed his eyes at me, picked the mug back up, and took a long gulp. I stared at him, wide-eyed, half-impressed and half-aghast.

"Bet you didn't see that coming," he said proudly.

"No, I didn't," I admitted. "Was that...enjoyable?"

"Not at all," Rouhr sputtered. "I deeply regret doing that. I just wanted to spite you."

"Aw, you're so loving." I rolled my eyes. He walked over to where I sat at my desk, bent down, and planted a huge kiss on my cheek.

"What's that?" He indicated the datapad covered by an expensive fabric sleeve that bore the emblem of the capital city.

"I don't know yet." I twisted in my seat to look at him. "I haven't had the chance to open it."

"Why not? It must be important if it's from the capital," Rouhr reasoned.

"It probably *is* important. That's why I wanted to wait for you so we could open it together," I explained.

"I'm here. What are you waiting for?" Rouhr took a few steps back to sit at the edge of our shared bed. I removed the fabric sleeve from the datapad and powered it on. It asked for a facial scan to ensure that I was the person who received it.

After the scan was completed and it had verified that the face it had scanned belonged to Vidia Birch, a letter appeared on the screen. I read it quickly.

"It's a job offer," I explained.

"Really?" Rouhr sounded surprised. "What's the job?"

"The city leaders of the capital want to meet with me," I continued reading. "They want me to take an active role in the rebuilding of the city."

"That sounds like quite an honor." Rouhr reached out and rubbed my shoulder. "What do you think?"

"There's no going back to Fraga," I sighed. There hadn't been enough of the town left after the Xathi attacks. The few survivors had resettled in other towns, rebuilding their lives the best they could.

"Glymna doesn't really need me, either," I mused. "I mostly just make sure everything continues to run smoothly and interject so I feel like I'm contributing."

"If they don't need you anymore, I think you should dedicate yourself to people who do," Rouhr said.

"I think you're right." I turned around with a sly grin on my face. "You know what that means?"

He looked confused for a moment before realization came over him. "No," he scowled. "We don't need to move."

"Rouhr!" I sighed. C

"We have the Gateway," Rouhr shrugged.

"I don't want to have to get Fen or Amira to open a rift through all of time and space just so I can go to a market," I laughed. "Besides, we could have an entire house instead of just a room."

"It's a nice room," Rouhr said defensively.

I climbed onto the mattress and sat behind him with one leg on either side of his. I wrapped my arms around his shoulders, despite the fact that they were almost too broad for my arms to fit all the way around.

"It's a very nice room," I hummed. "But what if we had more than one nice room? What if my office wasn't a foot from my bedroom?"

"I've lived on ships for over twenty years," he sighed. "I've grown so used to it, I don't think I'd be comfortable anywhere else."

"We can sleep here on weekends," I offered. "Like a reverse vacation."

"Very funny," Rouhr chuckled. "What would I even do if I lived in a human city?"

"I actually had some thoughts on that," I grinned.

"Why do those words fill me with dread?" he said wryly.

"Because you hate change," I teased. "Do you want to know my idea or not?"

"I want to know," Rouhr admitted.

"I was thinking you could work in the capital with me as a representative of the planet's new alien population," I said. "It wouldn't be all that different from being a general. You'd have to check in with your crew, get reports, and hold meetings. You love doing that kind of stuff!"

"I'm not much of a politician," Rouhr shook his head. "You told me once that it's like a dance, and I still don't know the steps."

"That's exactly why you should do it," I said enthusiastically. "No one would ever accuse you of corruption because you'll be above it. Your men and their needs will always come first."

"That's not true," Rouhr corrected me.

"What do you mean?" I asked, brow furrowed.

"You come first now." Rouhr reached back and pulled me around until I was in his lap. "You're always going to come first."

I melted in his arms. He lowered his head and pressed his lips to mine.

"If you don't want to take the job, I won't ask you to," I said when our lips parted.

"I'll consider it," he said. "After all, I'm technically

not working. There's nothing for me to be a general of here."

"We don't have a formal military," I said. "Perhaps you could form one."

"I think I'll let your planet take a break from war before I start recruiting troops," Rouhr chuckled.

"That's probably a good idea," I admitted. "Don't forget, it's your planet, too, now."

We sat together on the bed, wrapped in each other's arms long into the night. It didn't matter that we were breaking our new sleeping rules, we were too busy planning the future. Not just our own future, but the future of the planet.

Our planet.

And what a bright future it was.

LETTER FROM ELIN

Thank you so much for coming along with me for the first chapter of the Conquered World saga!

The Xathi might be defeated (for now) but don't worry, there will be plenty of new adventures for our valiant crew and their mates.

Besides, Jeneva was being pretty careful not to drink any alcohol at the party, don't you think? :)

There's a lot of fun waiting in the next chapter of the saga, and you can get started now with Karzin, book seven of the Conquered World! You can keep reading for a preview.

And please don't forget to leave a review. I love reading what you think of the books!

XOXO,

Elin

nnie

I USED to be a heavy sleeper. A bomb could go off and I wouldn't stir.

Then one day, a bomb did go off.

Now, the slightest noise brought me out of my slumber.

This morning, it was the soft sigh of my younger sister, Cassie, as she rolled over on her sleeping mat.

Usually, it was my older brother Helix that woke me. He often talked in his sleep. He used to be a city official in Duvest before the sky cracked open and everything changed.

Once I was awake, there was no going back to sleep.

I squinted across the room to the clock placed on the floor and sighed. I would've had to get up soon anyway. At least now I could take a little extra time with breakfast.

It was hard to move quietly in the house. It consisted of only two rooms, not including a washroom, and was built almost entirely of scrap. From the outside, our house looked like pieces of four different houses stitched together. One of our walls was entirely metal and slightly curved. Apparently, it came from the alien space ship that had defeated the Xathi.

Helix refused to touch that wall. His sleeping mat was placed as far away from it as it possibly could be. He didn't have anything against the aliens that had saved our planet.

He'd be a fool if he did. But he didn't like anything that reminded him of the Xathi.

Helix was on duty when the Xathi swarmed Duvest. He faced one head-on in order to give people a chance to escape. He survived, but only just. The Xathi took off the lower half of his left leg. Helix was retired from being a city official with the highest honors, but that hadn't helped him find work since.

The floor creaked under my feet. It wasn't a proper floor, just rows of flat-ish planks lined up next to each other to keeps us off the dirt. I heard my father snore in the other room. He and my mother used to own a general goods store. The Xathi destroyed that, too.

"Andromeda, be quiet," Cassie groaned. "I only got home an hour ago."

Andromeda was my full first name. I had no idea what possessed my mother to give me such a formal, old-fashioned name. For as long as I remembered, I'd insisted on going by Annie.

Cassie only called me Andromeda when she was in a foul mood, which was more often than not.

"That's not my fault, Cassiopeia," I snapped, invoking her equally awful first name in return. "What are you even doing out so late at night?"

"Pretending I live anywhere but here," she replied.

"If you got a job, you could live somewhere else," I replied.

"I guess I won't be sleeping in this morning," Helix groaned.

"Sorry, Helix," Cassie mumbled. She didn't mind vexing me, but she hated disrupting Helix.

"Any plans today?" I asked him.

"Liddy Burris is trying to open up a grocery on the other end of town. I'm going to offer to do her books," he replied.

"I think that would suit you," I smiled.

"Me, too," Cassie grinned. "Want some coffee?"

"I'm the oldest. Neither of you should be babying me," Helix chuckled.

"We don't baby you," Cassie said defensively.

Maybe we did baby him. A little.

"Cass, do you even know how to use the coffee maker?" Helix asked.

"Annie does." Cassie jerked her chin in my direction. I bought the coffee maker last week. The week before, I bought a hot plate and skillet. Both were placed on the floor in the corner farthest from our sleeping mats.

Next week, I wanted to buy a bigger food storage unit. The one we had now didn't keep perishables well enough. We couldn't afford to keep throwing away food. Rent was due next week, as well. It wasn't much. Everyone living in Somerst paid a monthly fee to keep the town running. I paid my own, as well as the fees for the rest of my family.

I opened the storage unit and pulled out three eggs. A quick sniff told me they were still edible but I would have to go to the market today after work. The cheese had gone bad overnight. That's what you got when you bought stuff that they were ready to throw out because it was the only thing you could afford.

I opened a window and tossed the cheese out onto the unpaved road. Somerst had yet to develop a suitable waste disposal system. The City of Nyheim offered to collect our waste for a fee, but everyone in Somerst agreed the fee was too high.

Councilwoman Vidia assured us she was working on a solution.

"Cheese is bad. But the bread is still good." I held up a bagged loaf of dark brown bread.

"I wouldn't call that bread good," Helix joked.

"It won't poison you," I corrected with a laugh. I'd met others who'd suffered injuries at the hands of the Xathi. Many were angry, many were sad. Helix always had a smile on his face. His sense of humor never faltered. He was my hero for that.

"That's all a man can ask for nowadays," he replied.

"Is there any butter?" Cassie asked.

"We finished it two days ago," I reminded her. "I'll pick more up tonight."

"Eggs and dry toast for breakfast then?" she grumbled. I ignored her as I cracked the eggs into the skillet and turned on the hot plate.

"I hope Liddy Burris does manage that grocery. The market in Nyheim is always so crowded."

"Go at a less busy time, then," Cassie suggested.

"I would, except I work, like so many others do," I sighed. "Why can't you get a job, again?"

"Nowhere will take me," Cass replied. "I've asked everyone in this heap of wreckage."

"This heap of wreckage is your home, Cass." Helix

had a warning tone in his voice. It was slight, but it was enough to get Cassie to change her tone.

"Not for long," she said. "We'll all move to a nice big house again. We'll all have our own rooms again."

"How about you ride into Nyheim with me? There's plenty of jobs there," I suggested. Cassie opened her mouth to speak. No doubt she had an excuse prepared in advanced, but Helix gave her a look.

"That's a good idea," Cass said.

She was in her first year of university when the Xathi attacked. The college still hadn't reopened.

"Maybe there's an opening at my lab," I said brightly.

"No offense, but you have the dullest job on the planet," Cass replied.

"The job isn't dull. My assignments are dull." I was a geologist in Nyheim. I had the least seniority out of all the other workers, so I always got the short end of the stick when it came to jobs. I didn't mind, though. I still got a decent paycheck.

"Still going to have to pass," Cass replied. "You're burning the eggs."

"I am not. I don't like runny eggs." I scrambled the eggs with a wooden spoon, except the spoon part broke off a few weeks ago.

"Take some off for me then." Cass grabbed one of our chipped plates. "I need something to soften the toast." I scrapped some gooey eggs onto her plate and placed a piece of bread on the part of the hotplate not covered by the skillet. Cass grabbed the bread before it was toasty and devoured everything on her plate in less than a minute.

"I'm going to wash up. I shouldn't smell like I slept on the floor when I apply for jobs," she declared.

"Don't use all the hot water," I warned her. After Cassie shut the door, I turned to Helix. "She's going to melt my brain."

"Remember, she's only known the cushy life. She didn't have to help mom and dad in the shop like we did," Helix said. Our parents' shop really took off when Cassie was five and too young to be useful. Helix and I spent most of our childhood sweeping, counting, and stocking. For most of Cassie's life, she'd wanted for nothing.

"She doesn't wear hardship well." I grabbed another plate and scooped a generous portion of eggs for Helix.

"Put some of mine back. There's not enough for you," he insisted.

"There's plenty for me," I replied. "Besides, I can always pick up something else in the city."

"You shouldn't have to," Helix said. "You do everything for us. The least we can do is give you the lion's share of breakfast."

"That would be silly, considering you're the lion of the family," I smiled.

"I still have no idea what a lion looks like," Helix laughed. That was one of the many inside jokes we shared as a family. Dad thought it was funny to use Earth expressions that made little sense here on Ankou. Don't wake the bear was a particular favorite of his.

"I think it has green scales and twenty eyes," I said.

"No way. A lion breathes fire and has three legs," he insisted.

"You win. Breathing fire is way cooler than twenty eyes," I admitted. Steam pouring from underneath the bathroom door caught my eye. I groaned and stood from my crouched position over the skillet.

"Cass, easy on the hot water!" I banged on the door.

"You're going to bring the walls down if you keep banging like that!" my mother called from the other room. I rolled my eyes and said nothing. I was well into my twenties, but that didn't stop my mother from scolding me like a toddler.

"I'm going to fetch more water," I told Helix. "Cass is bound to use it all. Can you watch my food?"

"You got it," Helix grinned.

I opened our flimsy front door and grabbed the bucket sitting just outside. Lucky for us, we lived close to the water dispensary. The line was long, but it moved quickly. We were only allowed to fill up one bucket at a time to make sure the well didn't run dry.

When I brought the filled bucket back to the house,

I dumped its contents into our water tank. Just as I thought, Cassie nearly used up all of it. Dad would need to get more.

When I went back into the house, Cassie was still in the shower. She must've planned this. She knew I wouldn't risk being late to work.

"Crap," I groaned. "I have to go."

"What about breakfast?" Helix asked.

"Just eat my eggs. I don't have time," I urged him. "Tell Cassie her plan worked."

KARZIN

"Pardon me, leader Karzin. You have guests."

I turned to see Pem, one of the Urai, standing behind me at the command center doors of the *Aurora*, his arms clasped behind his back.

"What do you mean, that I have guests? Who?" This was not something I wanted, nor had the patience for.

Pem, with a passive look of indifference, touched his speech pad with his left hand. "They are members of your strike team. They have come to speak with you."

With a nod, he turned and fairly floated out of the command center. Despite living with them, I was still bewildered by the way they moved, so smoothly, effortlessly, and fluidly.

With a string of curses that had become part of my

regular vocabulary, I left the command center and headed to meet the team. I crossed over the open-air bridge back into the middle section of the ship and passed by a mirror.

I stopped. My long hair was gone, I had chopped most of it off months ago. Now, it was a disheveled clump that reminded me of a bird's nest. My once clean-shaven face was filled with three days of stubble, and even my purple shoulder bands seemed to be losing their luster. I stormed away from the mirror, if the men couldn't deal with how I looked, then it didn't matter to me.

They were waiting for me in what had become the common area when anyone returned to the *Aurora*.

Iq'her, with his bright green circuitry shining along his bald scalp down along his arms, sat in one of the chairs, playing with his knife.

Sylor, the one that would be my second, my cousin, at least in species, leaned against a wall, his green skin matching the large plant he was studying.

Then, the brothers. Rokul and his silent brashness, Takar and his attempt to show himself as a sophisticated, well-educated man, both standing in the center of the room, watching the hall which I entered from. Their matching reddish-orange skin shone in the light, their scalps still shaved everywhere but in the middle, where they both insisted on spiking it from front to back.

"What is it? I'm busy," I said as I entered the common area and leaned on a table. Unless this was a mission, I had no interest in what they had to say.

"Ah, the 'I'm busy' claim that you have been so apt to use these months," Takar scoffed.

I looked at him for a single moment, then turned my attention to Sylor. "Why are you here? Is there something that needs to be done?"

The look he gave me showed concern, and anger. "We need to talk, about you."

Of course. "What is there to talk about? I'm doing my job while the four of you are off doing whatever it is that humans do."

Sylor left his position by the plant and approached me. His left hand, forever mangled in a long-ago attack by the Xathi, twitched slightly. "That's the problem. You look at us as though we have forgotten who and what we are."

"Haven't you?" I was loud and didn't care. They, and the others, had forgotten where we come from, and what happened to us, to our peoples, to our families. "Haven't you forgotten what's happened and is still happening? But, instead of looking for a way to get off the planet and return home, you've decided to 'settle' here and forget everything."

"We haven't forgotten. Nothing can make us forget," Takar started.

I wasn't going to let him lie to me. "Don't give me that!" I yelled. "Don't you *dare* tell me that you haven't forgotten. You, your brother, the rest of the entire crew have given up!" A bit of spittle flew from my mouth as I spoke, so I wiped my mouth.

I could see the anger growing in Takar.

"You dare accuse us of forgetting and giving up? We," he pointed between his brother and himself, "lost family to the Xathi, as well. And," he said, his voice calming and growing quiet, "unlike you, we know that our family is dead. We watched them die before our eyes. The idea that there are still Xathi *anywhere* in the universe boils my blood and angers me, but I have also come to learn that, at the moment, there is nothing that can be done by our hands. My brother and I have not forgotten, we have merely moved on, for now."

I looked between them all. Rokul nodded, Iq'her looked more interested in his knife, and Sylor crossed his arms as he looked at me. "What you're trying to say to me, is that you're…what…waiting for the right moment to find a way back home?"

Rokul shook his head and took a seat. Sylor simply stared at me, and Takar walked away, leaving the room.

It was Iq'her, in his formal tones, that answered my question. "What they are trying to say, sir, is that we are trying to make the best of the situation that is at hand. You, of all people, sir, should understand that there are times when you must step back in order to better fortify a position or to better assess a situation."

"Oh, so this is a strategic thing? Is that it?" I knew they were trying to move me, to...how did the humans say it...con me. They were saying what they thought needed to be said in order to sway me.

With a movement quicker than I could follow, Iq'her put his knife away and shot to his feet. He was in front of me, in my face, rage in his eyes. "I have followed you, I have listened to you, I have respected you like no other person in my life. It was you that saved me from my own darkness, and you speak to me in this way. You are no longer the man, no longer the leader, that I knew. You are a fool."

I shoved him away from me as hard as I could. "I'm the fool? Me?! I'm the only one that's still looking for a way home! I'm the only one that still cares!"

That might have been over the line. The pain in Iq'her's eyes was mirrored on Rokul's face. Sylor stared at the ceiling, his shoulders sagging. I didn't care. "I'm the only one..."

"Still trying?" Sylor finished for me. "You were about to say that, correct? You're the one that has given up." He walked towards me, put his hand on Iq'her's shoulder and gently pulled him away.

When Iq'her went back to his seat, Sylor took his place in front of me. "You've locked yourself away here, for weeks, months on end. You refuse to leave, you refuse to acknowledge that, at least for now, Ankou is our home, and refuse to accept the fact that when we left our homes, the Xathi were unstoppable."

"There is a chance that our homes have been destroyed and nothing is left of them," Takar said as he came back into the room. "The Xathi were...relentless and savage in their attacks. I know that there was nothing left of our own world when they were finished."

I knew that Takar and Rokul were from one of the secondary systems in Skotan space. Few of those planets had survived the initial Xathi attack.

Sylor, with a short nod, turned back to me. "Their attack upon Valorn was devastating. We were already losing, badly. There is a chance that the fight there has already been lost."

I had had enough. I was finished with them.

"Then you have forgotten how strong our people really are. *True* Valorni do not give up the battle, and I refuse to forget our people, our families, or what our responsibility is. If you have nothing else for me except useless comments about my actions or my behavior, then I suggest you leave, now," I growled.

"No. We're here to fix whatever this is and get the

real Karzin back," Rokul said from his chair. "We need you back, sir."

I shook my head, waved them off, and left the common area. "You know how to leave," I called back behind me. I returned to the command center and finished working on the defective computer core. I needed to get it back into space, back to the satellite it had come from, and back to work on finding a signal.

While I worked, I watched them leave through one of the outer surveillance cameras. They opened a rift and walked through, the rift closing behind them.

It was about time they left, they had wasted enough of my time.

If they couldn't understand what I was doing, I wanted nothing to do with them. I needed to put my concentration into this.

"Leader Karzin?" It was Pem,again. I turned to look at him. "Might I ask you a question?"

"Fine. What is it?"

He walked closer to me, his left hand on his speech-box. "Your men seem to be...very passionate about your current state of affairs."

"What of it?"

"I was curious as to why you and your men have such a differing set of opinions. Do you not believe in your cause upon this world?"

"Our *cause*, as you put it, is over. The Xathi have

been destroyed here and the humans are safe. It's time
we return home, to *our* home. That is my cause now."

"And if there is no way to return to your home?" he
asked.

I never answered him.

Because it simply wasn't an option.

I couldn't let it be.

ANNIE

Thanks to Cassie's little stunt, I was running late. I
didn't get to shower before work. I barely got to run a
comb through my hair and brush my teeth. My nice
pants were wrinkled after hanging on the line to dry.
My stomach growled in protest to skipping breakfast
and my minimalist dinner the night before.

I jumped on the shuttle seconds before the doors
closed. There were no seats, but that was normal. I
grabbed on to the first solid, non-living thing I felt just
as the shuttle took off. Most of the seats were filled by
people just like me, harried and trying to get to work.

A few of the passengers were of alien species. The
first time I saw one riding the shuttle, I couldn't stop
staring. I felt so rude, but I couldn't help it. I'd never
been that close to an alien before. Now, though I was
still curious about them, I was more used to the sight.

There were three separate species of aliens that now

lived alongside us. There were the Skotan, red from head to toe with some kind of retractable scales, though I'd never seen them in person. K'ver were gray and appeared to have circuits embedded directly into their skin. Two of them had taken jobs at my lab in the tech innovations department. I smiled to them in passing but I'd yet to have a chance to speak to one. The Valorni were green and built like barns. I saw them the least out of all the species. Their natural strength made them ideal for labor-oriented jobs. It was likely that a Valorni built the house I lived in now.

Some still treated the aliens with skepticism, but I saw no reason to. If they wanted to do us harm, they wouldn't have risked so much to save our world from the Xathi. I'd heard they couldn't leave the planet now. They'd trapped themselves here to save us.

That earned each one of them respect in my book.

The shuttle ride was brief, but I still had a distance to walk until I reached my office.

Nyheim used to be spectacular. In a way, it still was, but it was a beauty of the spirit, not the eye. It had survived so much and still stood strong. Most of its memorable structures were gone now.

Bare bones of buildings in disrepair lined the streets. It was more like walking through a skeleton of a city than an actual city.

Halfway between the shuttle station and my office

was a tiny eatery made out of a dislodged shipping container. Orlin, the owner, furnished the inside with a small kitchen and cut windows in the sides to take orders.

"How's it going, Annie?" he asked when I stepped up to the window. "Cassie make you late again?"

"You know it," I sighed. Because of Cassie, I was forced to grab breakfast from Orlin at least once a week. I didn't mind, though. Orlin was a fantastic cook. He could make even meal rations taste high class.

"Have you told her I'm hiring?" he asked. "I'm getting too old to be working here every day."

"You're not getting old," I said with a dismissive wave. Orlin was barely fifty and in great shape for his age. Though I could understand wanting a day off every now and then. I was going on my twelfth day straight. "I almost got her on the shuttle today. If I told her I wanted her to work here, she'd never come. I have to trick her somehow."

"Good luck with that," Orlin chuckled. "Your usual, then?"

"Please." I reached into my back to pull out my credit chip, but Orlin waved me off.

"You've got enough to worry about. I'm not going to make you worry about food on top of it all," he said.

"Thanks, Orlin," I grinned. I stood off to the side while Orlin made a fresh pot of coffee and flakey croissant with egg, cheese, butter, *and* a small piece bacon. If Cassie knew, I bet she'd change her tune about coming to the city with me. We never had enough to afford bacon on top of our regular groceries. Meat had become a rarity since most of the domesticated animals were killed or escaped during the Xathi invasion and many of the wild creatures moved to other areas.

Orlin handed me my coffee and food. I flashed him another grateful smile before continuing on my way. The croissant was devoured by the time I reached my building.

The top half of my office building was gone. A tarp was stretched over the gap to make a ceiling, but no one used that floor anyway. My lab was on the third floor, untouched by the Xathi ship during its initial crash landing.

I was lucky to have this job. My last place of employment closed down not long after the Xathi ship crashed onto our planet. I applied to my current job, expecting nothing, but I was pleasantly surprised. All of the sciences were in demand as everyone scrambled to get back to pre-war levels of industry.

I'd barely stepped into the room when one of my colleagues ran up to me. Bea was a woman in her mid-thirties who always wore her black hair in a bun so tight I couldn't imagine how it wasn't painful for her. She had yet to speak to me at all since I started working here. Honestly, no one here had been very social, so if Bea was running up to me, either something terrible or something fantastic had happened.

"You've got to see this!" she exclaimed. "I've never seen anything like it."

"What?" I asked. Bea grabbed my arm and tugged me through the lobby of the building.

"I came into the main labs, yeah? And all I could hear were these piercing beeps and alarms," she spoke quickly.

"A malfunction, then?" I asked.

"That's what I thought! Especially once I realized they were coming from your station, no offense," she looked over her shoulder and shot me a look of apology.

"My station?" I stammered. I could understand her surprise. My station was always silent.

I'd been assigned a task that initially sounded interesting. My job was to monitor the area around the remains of the half of the Xathi ship that had crashed back down to the planet's surface. I traveled out to the wreckage myself and placed all sorts of scanners and monitors on the surface of the earth and beneath it at various intervals.

The main concern was unknown substances leaking from the Xathi ship and negatively affecting the soil around it. Though, since the Xathi ship's remains were far out in the desert, where no humans had ever settled, there wasn't much of a risk factor. It was mainly for scientific curiosity.

I thought it was going to be such an exciting job. I thought I'd be at the forefront of discoveries, unveiling the mysteries of the giant crystal insects that attacked us. However, it had been nearly two months and nothing had happened yet.

Until now, apparently.

"I'm sure it was just a glitch," I said lamely.

"I checked!" Bea cried. "I assumed it was a glitch, too. Again, no offense."

"None taken," I muttered.

"There's nothing wrong with any of your consoles. All of your monitors are in working order but they're recording stuff that's off the charts. Literally!" Bea dragged me into the elevator and pushed the button for our floor at least twenty times before the doors closed.

"How many caffeine pills have you had today, Bea?" I asked. I once saw a whole bottle of caffeine tablets at her station. It wasn't uncommon for everyone, other than me, to work late into the night on their various assignments.

"I've been here for nearly twenty-four hours," Bea said.

"What? That's not healthy!" I exclaimed.

"I have so much to finish up! Didn't I tell you? I'm

transferring at the end of the week," she replied. I wanted to tell her that since she'd never spoken to me before now that of course she didn't tell me she was transferring, but I refrained.

"You're transferring?" I asked.

"My husband got a job in Kaster. It pays too well for us to say no," she explained. If she kept talking as fast as she was, she was going to bite her tongue clean off.

"Is there much work for a botanist in Kaster?" I asked, praying that she actually was a botanist.

"There's lots of work for botanists everywhere nowadays," she replied.

I tried not to audibly sigh with relief. "The Xathi did a number on the local plant life. There's so much to study, I'll have my hands full for months. Bet you wish you'd studied botany now, don't you?" She nudged me playfully and cackled a little too loudly.

"Promise me you won't take any more of those pills, okay?" I patted her shoulder.

"Don't worry, I've emptied the bottle."

"That makes me more worried," I winced.

The world's slowest elevator finally arrived at our floor. Bea dragged me out of the elevator and through the double doors of the main lab. I heard the beeping alarms before we entered the room. I half expected the alarms to be nothing more than a side effect of Bea's excessive caffeine intake.

"See? It's going at it again!" she exclaimed.

"Please sit down," I urged. "I'm worried you're going to have a heart attack."

My station was in the farthest corner of the room. All of the monitors I'd placed out in the desert corresponded to a light on my console. All of them were flashing green, a sign of change in the environment.

"What could this be?" I muttered to myself as I approached the console. The first thing I noticed was that all of the monitors were no longer where I'd placed them. They'd been shifted considerably. Some looked like they were buried far deeper than I'd left them. That could've only happened if the earth itself had shifted.

I pulled up a seismograph that reflected any changes in the amount of energy coursing through the planet's crust. The graph showed that huge spikes of energy had been bursting from the earth all night.

"So, what's happening?" Bea appeared at my side, startling me.

"I don't know," I replied. "But something out there is causing tremors bigger than anything I've ever seen."

GET KARZIN NOW!

https://elinwynbooks.com/conquered-world-alien-romance/

PLEASE DON'T FORGET TO LEAVE A REVIEW!

Readers rely on your opinions, and your review can help others decide on what books they read. Make sure your opinion is heard and leave a review where you purchased this book!

Don't miss a new release! You can sign up for release alerts at both Amazon and Bookbub:
bookbub.com/authors/elin-wyn
amazon.com/author/elinwyn

For a free short story, opportunities for advance review copies, release news and the occasional cat picture, please join the newsletter!
https://elinwynbooks.com/newsletter-signup/

And don't forget the Facebook group, where I post sneak peeks of chapters and covers!

https://www.facebook.com/groups/ElinWyn/

DON'T MISS THE STAR BREED!

Given: Star Breed Book One

When a renegade thief and a genetically enhanced mercenary collide, space gets a whole lot hotter!

Thief Kara Shimsi has learned three lessons well - keep her head down, her fingers light, and her tithes to the syndicate paid on time.

But now a failed heist has earned her a death sentence - a one-way ticket to the toxic Waste outside the dome. Her only chance is a deal with the syndicate's most ruthless enforcer, a wolfish mountain of genetically-modified muscle named Davien.

The thought makes her body tingle with dread-or is it heat?

Mercenary Davien has one focus: do whatever is necessary to get the credits to get off this backwater mining colony and back into space. The last thing he wants is a smart-mouthed thief - even if she does have the clue he needs to hunt down whoever attacked the floating lab he and his created brothers called home.

Caring is a liability. Desire is a commodity. And love could get you killed.

https://elinwynbooks.com/star-breed/

ABOUT THE AUTHOR

I love old movies – *To Catch a Thief*, *Notorious*, *All About Eve* — and anything with Katherine Hepburn in it. Clever, elegant people doing clever, elegant things.

I'm a hopeless romantic.

And I love science fiction and the promise of space.

So it makes perfect sense to me to try to merge all of those loves into a new science fiction world, where dashing heroes and lovely ladies have adventures, get into trouble, and find their true love in the stars!